# THE GOOD DOG

**Don't miss these other books by Avi!**

*Bright Shadow*
*The Christmas Rat*
*Silent Movie*
*Traitor's Gate*
*Wolf Rider*

# THE GOOD DOG

A Richard Jackson Book
Atheneum Books for Young Readers
New York  London  Toronto  Sydney

ATHENEUM BOOKS FOR YOUNG READERS

An imprint of Simon & Schuster Children's Publishing Division

1230 Avenue of the Americas, New York, New York 10020

This book is a work of fiction. Any references to historical events, real people, or real locales are used fictitiously. Other names, characters, places, and incidents are products of the author's imagination, and any resemblance to actual events or locales or persons, living or dead, is entirely coincidental.

Copyright © 2001 by Avi

All rights reserved, including the right of reproduction in whole or in part in any form.

ATHENEUM BOOKS FOR YOUNG READERS is a registered trademark of Simon & Schuster, Inc.

For information about special discounts for bulk purchases, please contact Simon & Schuster Special Sales at 1-866-506-1949 or business@simonandschuster.com.

The Simon & Schuster Speakers Bureau can bring authors to your live event. For more information or to book an event, contact the Simon & Schuster Speakers Bureau at 1-866-248-3049 or visit our website at www.simonspeakers.com.

Also available in an Atheneum Books for Young Readers hardcover edition

Book design by Michael Nelson

The text for this book is set in Perpetua.

Manufactured in the United States of America

0210 OFF

First paperback edition April 2003

20 19 18 17 16 15

The Library of Congress has cataloged the hardcover edition as follows:

Avi, 1937–

The good dog / by Avi.

p. cm.

Summary: McKinley, a malamute, is torn between the domestic world of his human family and the wild world of Lupin, a wolf that is trying to recruit dogs to replenish the dwindling wolf pack.

1. Dogs—Juvenile fiction. [1. Dogs—Fiction. 2. Wolves—Fiction.] I. Title.

PZ10.3.A965   Go   2001

[Fic]—dc21          00-53600

ISBN 978-0-689-83824-8 (hc)

ISBN 978-0-689-83825-5 (pbk)

*For Jack and McKinley, the real ones*

# THE GOOD DOG

"Dad! Ma! McKinley! Guess what I saw!"

McKinley had been sleeping in the front yard bushes. Hearing the familiar voice, he lifted his head and looked around with sleepy eyes. He was just in time to see Jack, his human pup, skid so fast on his mountain bike that gravel scattered everywhere. The boy leaped off the bike, raced across the place where the cars sat, and ran into the house.

Now what? McKinley wondered.

Though he would have liked to sleep more, McKinley stood, yawned, stretched his muscles until they were tight, then relaxed them until they were loose. Shaking his head, he jangled his collar tags, and then ambled toward the house.

By the time McKinley reached the door, it had already swung shut. As he had taught himself to do, he bent down, wedged a large forepaw where there was a gap beneath the door, extended his claws, and pushed. The door popped open a little.

Sticking his nose into the gap, McKinley shoved the door further open and squirmed inside. Once there, he sniffed. Smelling dinner, he trotted down the hallway, wagging his tail, till he heard Jack saying, "Dad, I'm not making it up. I really saw a wolf."

McKinley stopped short. His tail drooped. Was that the *wolf* word the boy had used?

When he was young—Jack had also been much younger—McKinley had spotted a wolf during a walk with his people. It was just a glimpse, but the people had seen it, too. They had become very excited. That's when McKinley learned the *wolf* word. He could recall the wolf's reek, a mix of deep woods, dark earth, and fresh meat. Its wildness had frightened him. And excited him. But that was a long time ago.

Wide awake now, McKinley hurried past the large room and into the small food place.

Jack was talking to the man of the family. Sometimes the man was called Dad, sometimes Gil. McKinley liked him and the way he always smelled of the outdoors.

"Now, hang on, Jack," the man said. "You sure it wasn't just a big old German shepherd? They can look a lot like a wolf."

McKinley stood still, his head cocked. There it was again, the *wolf* word.

"No way, Dad," the human pup answered. "You know how much I've read about wolves. I'm sure this was one. I mean, yeah, at first I thought it was McKinley. But it wasn't."

Wanting to understand more, McKinley jumped onto one of the sitting places near where the humans put their food when they ate. Mouth slightly open, tail wagging, he sat, turning from the pup to the man as each spoke.

"I'm not saying you're wrong," the man said. "Just, if you're right, it's pretty amazing. Hasn't been a wolf sighted around here for years. Remember the time we spotted one up in the Zirkel Wilderness? But not here in Steamboat Springs."

McKinley saw Jack look around. "Where's Mom?"

At the mention of Jack's female—the boy called her Mom, the man called her Sarah—McKinley barked once. The woman spent time on Most Cars Way in a place where there was lots of food, and often brought him treats—like bones.

Gil said, "She has to work the dinner shift. So it'll be just you and me tonight. Sausages and carrots. And your mom made bread. Now keep talking as you set the table."

Jack all but threw down his eating sticks and tall, clear bowls as he chattered. "I was a little scared," he was saying. "I mean, that wolf really surprised me. I think I surprised him, too."

The human pup poured water for himself and the man into the tall bowls, then thumped down onto the sitting place. McKinley edged closer to the boy.

"Here's grub," the man said as he brought food to the boy and sat across from him. "And I'm starving."

McKinley, eyeing the food, drooled and licked his own nose.

"I was marking trail up by Rabbit Ears Pass all day," the man said. "Fair amount of snow up there already. Promises a good season."

"Hear that, McKinley?" Jack cried. "Snow is coming!"

*Snow,* a word McKinley knew and loved. He barked in appreciation.

"But go on," the man said to the pup. "Tell me exactly what you saw."

Jack spoke between mouthfuls. "See—the wolf had this thick, gray fur coat—with sort of flecks of gold. His head was wide—his muzzle was light colored—and I think he had a limp."

"Was he bigger than McKinley?"

Jack turned toward him. McKinley, wishing the human pup would calm down and speak slower, leaned over and licked his face.

"A lot skinnier," Jack said, wiping his cheek with

the back of a hand. "Longer legs, too. Gray fur. Not blackish."

"You didn't see a collar, did you?"

"No way."

"Describe his eyes."

McKinley watched closely as Jack swallowed the last of the sausage. "Not, you know, brown and round like McKinley's. Like, sort of yellowish. And, you know, egg-shaped."

The man reached for his tall bowl and drank. Then he said, "Well, that's certainly wolflike. Where'd you see him?"

"Up in Strawberry Park."

McKinley yawned with nervousness. Strawberry Park was a small valley outside of Steamboat Springs. It was hemmed in by forested hills, and beyond, by snow-peaked mountains. Looming over everything was the great mountain, where most of the humans did their snow sliding.

There were only a few houses in the area, and the dogs who lived there ran completely free. McKinley was head dog there as well as in town.

"What were you doing there?" Gil asked.

Jack shrugged. "School was out. I was exploring."

"McKinley with you?"

Jack gave his dog a quick smile. "Wish he was."

Liking the attention, McKinley barked.

"Hey, how about feeding him his dinner?"

"McKinley, I'm sorry!"

The pup leaped up.

McKinley watched as Jack snatched his food bowl from the floor, then reached into a food box. The boy put some bits into the bowl, added water, and set it back on the ground. As a final touch, he placed two dog biscuits on top.

McKinley wagged his tail, jumped off the sitting place, and went for the wet food, gulping down the biscuits first.

"Jack," Gil said, "if that was a wolf—and I'm not saying it wasn't—there are going to be lots of people in town stirred up. Generally speaking, folks don't like wolves."

McKinley stopped eating to look around. There it was again, the *wolf* word.

"I know, Dad," Jack said. "People say wolves are mean and vicious. They aren't. Look at McKinley."

"McKinley is a malamute," Gil said. "Not a wolf."

"Part wolf," Jack insisted.

"Well, maybe so, way back. Not now. Look Jack, the point is, this is still ranching country. If people learn there's a wolf nearby, some of them will be wanting to hunt it down. Kill it. I'm serious, Jack. Since you like wolves, be smart. Don't let anybody know what you saw."

The words *hunt* and *kill* unsettled McKinley. Hunting was not something that Jack's family did. But there were many humans in town—and their dogs—who hunted. For McKinley it meant *danger*. Just the sense of it made him bark.

Jack and Gil turned to look at him.

Gil asked, "What do you think he's saying?"

"Wish I knew," Jack said.

**2**

Food bowl emptied, McKinley trotted back down the hallway. Finding the front door shut, he stood up on his rear legs. He mouthed the doorknob, twisted it, pulled the door open a bit, quickly nosed the door open further, then went out onto the deserted way.

From where he sat he could look into the front yards of many houses. Tree leaves had fallen. Bushes had thinned. The air was ripe with autumn smells.

McKinley sniffed for Aspen, his best friend who lived next door. She was a retriever whose gentle eyes had always appealed to him. The two dogs spent lots of time together.

She did not seem to be around.

Sitting quietly, McKinley put his mind to the words he had just heard. As he understood them, his human pup had seen a wolf in Strawberry Park. And there had been talk of hunting—killing, too.

McKinley sighed with frustration. He had been very young when he had come into Jack's house, a good place where he had plenty of food. The house was warm, too, which was important because for much of the year nights were cold and the ground snowy. His human pup had called him McKinley, not that the dog knew why. What he did know was that Jack was supposed to feed him twice a day, morning and night. In return, it was McKinley's responsibility to look after the three humans, protecting them—the boy in particular—and their home. He took his job seriously.

Of all the people in town, Jack—and the man and woman—were the humans McKinley knew best. Hardly a wonder that over the years he had come to understand some of their talk. He could grasp more meanings by watching faces and gestures, especially Jack's. Still, McKinley wished he understood more. It was frustrating taking care of them when, like tonight, their words were so difficult to understand.

Thinking that perhaps the dogs along Most Cars Way might have heard about a wolf, McKinley took off. At the first corner he stopped. He had caught sight of a piece of paper on a post. McKinley gazed up at it.

# LOST!

GREYHOUND
ANSWERS TO THE NAME OF
## DUCHESS
$200 REWARD!
CALL RALPH PYCRAFT
555-1678

McKinley had seen enough papers like this one to understand that a dog had run away and his human wanted him back. And McKinley recognized this dog. A member of the town pack, her person called her Duchess. What's more, McKinley could easily guess why she had run away, and knew why she should remain free. The human she lived with, a man called Pycraft, was famously mean to dogs.

Before, when Duchess ran off, she went to the boulders up in Strawberry Park. All McKinley could think was, Why hadn't she stayed there that first time?

He was about to continue on when two humans approached the pole. A dog—on a leash—was with them.

McKinley recognized the people as the Sullivans of Pine Smell Way. The dog was a big setter called Redburn, who lived with them. Taller than McKinley, slim and graceful, he was perfectly groomed, fur always seeming to have been just brushed. He trotted with perfection, too, head high, tail extended, leg feathers flowing. Redburn expected admiring glances—from humans and dogs alike.

McKinley sniffed the group. All three smelled of soap. They always did.

The humans stopped to look at the paper. Redburn acted as if McKinley wasn't there. Since McKinley was head dog, this was a clear snub.

"Duchess, eh?" the male Sullivan said, looking at the paper on the pole. "Cute-looking pooch."

"Must be something special if Ralph is offering a reward," the female Sullivan said. "The guy isn't exactly generous."

The man laughed. "Yeah, right. But if anyone can track that dog down, Redburn can. Don't you think so, fella?" He patted the setter on his head. The dog licked his hand.

Disgusted, McKinley wrinkled his nose and looked the other way. There was something about Redburn that he always found irritating.

"Be nice to get the money," the woman said. "Why don't you call Ralph?"

"I think I will."

As the three of them began to stroll away, Redburn, still ignoring McKinley, tossed his head high.

Too annoyed to respond, McKinley watched them go. His ears had pricked up at the word *Duchess*. Because the setter had a reputation for tracking skills, and since the people were looking at the paper—had even used the word *track*—McKinley tried to make sense of what he'd heard. He decided that the Sullivans were going to use Redburn to find Duchess. It figured. Sometimes, McKinley thought, it seemed Redburn acted as if he would have preferred being a human.

McKinley stood stiff-legged, shifted his ears forward, and lowered his tail. He was thinking a thought that often came to him: Why did humans think they owned their dogs when dogs only rarely thought they owned people? Sure, dogs and people lived together. The way McKinley saw it, they needed each other. But no dog should have to live with a human who treated her the way Pycraft did. Tied up in a yard. Forced to sleep in a doghouse made of hard, airless stuff. As far as McKinley was concerned, Duchess had every right to run off.

He was still gazing after the Sullivans and thinking hard when he heard a bark. He looked around. From out of the bushes peered Tubbs, a basset hound who lived at the corner of McKinley's way. With his big muzzle, deep-set eyes, long, droopy ears, and stubby legs, no one—neither dogs nor humans—took Tubbs very seriously.

He looked up and down the way. "Redburn gone?" Growling, McKinley nodded toward the paper.

Tubbs looked up. "You know me, McKinley, all nose, no eyes. Anything important?"

McKinley made a low grunt. "Duchess has taken off."

"Again?"

"Only this time I'm pretty sure Pycraft wants to track her down. And I think the Pine Smell Way Sullivans are getting Redburn to do it."

"Redburn! Oh, wow! That dog has a great nose. I mean, he and Sullivan go hunting all the time. What are you going to do about it?"

"Not sure. Guess I better let Duchess know."

"How do you do that?"

"Go up to Strawberry Park. Last time she hid out in the boulders."

"Wish her luck from me."

Tubbs—long tail wagging—waddled away.

McKinley knew why Tubbs assumed he should be the one to help Duchess. The Steamboat pack expected him to take charge of problems. He either provided successful leadership and protected their freedoms, or he would not be head dog for long.

McKinley turned, lifted a leg, and peed on the pole to inform the other dogs he had seen the paper about Duchess. If they didn't know he knew, they'd be coming by at all hours to bring him the news.

That done, McKinley headed downtown. Along Most Cars Way he came upon several dogs visiting the crowded food places. They met, sniffed each other, frolicked some. There was the usual exchange of gossip: who chased who, what this or that human did, the trouble some dog got into.

But most of the conversations were about Duchess and how she had run off.

No one mentioned a wolf. Nor did McKinley. By the time he completed his rounds he was sure there was no wolf. Jack must have made a mistake.

McKinley glanced up. The dark sky told him he'd spent more time downtown than he had intended. He needed to make sure his pup was in his sleeping place.

Under his breath, McKinley allowed himself a growl. It was always hard to take care of the pack and his humans at the same time. Dealing with Duchess would have to wait.

After letting himself in at home, McKinley lapped up some water from his bowl, then trotted to Jack's room. The boy was in his sleeping place, a block of staring papers in his hand.

"Hey, McKinley," Jack cried. "Where you been?"

McKinley wagged his tail and let himself be patted on the head.

Jack held up his staring papers. "Look at this book, boy. It's all about wolves."

Sure enough, on one side of the papers was a picture of a wolf's head.

McKinley gazed at it and whimpered.

"Hey, don't you like wolves? They're your relatives."

McKinley barked.

"Come on up here, boy," Jack said, tapping his soft sleeping place. "I'll protect you."

McKinley jumped up and lay down, head resting on the same lump of softness where his pup put his head.

Rolling over, Jack whispered into McKinley's ear: "Hey, McKinley, guess what? I'm thinking about finding that wolf."

McKinley lifted his head. There it was again, the *wolf* word. He gazed into the pup's eyes.

"I mean, wouldn't it be cool to live with wolves for a while? Like in *Julie of the Wolves*. Or *The Jungle Books*. But, you know, not forever. Just awhile."

McKinley wondered why the boy was talking

so much about wolves when there were none around.

"The only two problems," Jack continued, "I'm sure Mom and Dad wouldn't let me. And I'd have to do it before snow sets in. So don't tell them what I'm thinking, okay?" He gave McKinley a kiss on the snout.

"Can I ask you something?" Jack asked suddenly.

McKinley stared into the pup's eyes.

"How come when you lick my face, you always lick my cheeks, not my nose?"

Not waiting for an answer, Jack flopped down on his back.

With a yawn that was half nervous, half sleepiness, McKinley settled again onto the soft white lump and shut his eyes.

"I'm serious about finding that wolf, McKinley," Jack insisted as he reached up and clicked off the light. "I really am."

McKinley, still wondering what the boy was talking about, drifted off to sleep.

# 3

Next morning, a well-fed McKinley waited until Jack biked to his regular meeting of human pups. Then he himself headed for Strawberry Park.

Two ways led to the valley. One of them McKinley knew as Horse Smell Way. The other was called Porcupine Way. Nestled between the two was the many-doored place where, on most days, human pups got together.

McKinley truly liked young humans, enjoyed playing and going on outings while taking care of them. Even so, he was glad that, as he passed by this morning, the pups were in their special house. Duchess's hideaway needed to remain secret.

After trotting along for a while—staying to one side of Horse Smell Way to avoid cars—McKinley took a turn onto Cow Pen Way. It wound steeply up toward the high wilderness country—Buffalo Pass—a place he rarely visited.

But before going very far, McKinley turned onto Fox Haven Way, which was so muddy during the wet time after the snow that deep water ditches had been cut along the sides. McKinley stopped at the smallest house in the valley. Only during snow season did people come there. So the area around the cabin was almost entirely free of their smells. That was the reason local dogs used it to leave messages.

Behind the little house ran a creek. When hot weather came it was one of the best places to take a cooling swim after a ramble.

McKinley sniffed the trunk of a small aspen tree in front of the cabin. It grew where people stopped their cars. There he found exactly what he'd hoped to find. Duchess had left her mark in the dirt nearby—recently.

Barking with satisfaction, McKinley put his nose to the ground and trotted across the way, leaped over a ditch, and passed on into a field. He was headed toward the foothills and the woods. Here, thick groves of pine, aspen, and scrub oak grew. The smell of damp earth, moldy leaves, and decaying berries filled the air. Even so, Duchess's scent was easy to follow.

McKinley was well into the hills when he stopped in his tracks. He sniffed deeply. An entirely new scent was mixed in with the one Duchess had left. Leaning forward, tail extended tensely, McKinley ransacked his memory of smells. Suddenly, he knew what he was smelling. A wolf. A female wolf. Jack *had* seen one!

McKinley pulled back his ears, wrinkled his nose, and hunched his trembling body lower to the ground. Heart thumping, he thrust his nose directly into the wolf's scent. The smell was somewhat older than Duchess's, which meant the wolf had been here first. Perhaps she had gone on.

Tension easing, McKinley stood erect. The stiff black hairs along his back flattened. He lifted his tail. Once again he went forward but—this time—with caution.

Farther up into the hills—behind an open meadow of low grass—sat a circle of large boulders. During the summer, snakes sometimes gathered there. At first glance the boulders seemed wedged tightly together. But McKinley knew they concealed a cavelike chamber, a perfect den. To get in or out a dog needed only to crawl through a passage tunneled under one boulder. Duchess's trail led directly to that crevice.

Drawing closer, McKinley sniffed deeply. The wolf scent had intensified. Then he saw that the hole under the boulder had been enlarged to accommodate an animal bigger than Duchess. But though the wolf's smell certainly lingered, Duchess's scent was stronger. McKinley felt convinced that the wolf was no longer near.

Presenting himself in as friendly a way as possible, he lifted his rump, lowered his forepaws, raised his tail and, with his mouth open and tongue exposed, gave a friendly bark.

A short, sharp yelp came from among the boulders. The next moment Duchess popped out of the entry passage.

Smaller and thinner than McKinley, Duchess's strong, sleek greyhound body was covered with short fur. Her muzzle was long and narrow, her large eyes liquid. Small ears were constantly in motion as they responded warily to the slightest sounds.

As soon as Duchess crept from the hole, she took up the proper posture for greeting the head dog—ears back, tongue extended, one paw raised. She kept her tail low, wagging it slightly, averting her eyes.

McKinley, gazing down at Duchess, wagged his tail gently, and approached.

The two dogs touched noses, then sniffed each other's bodies to discover where they had been, with whom they had visited. McKinley noted that the wolf's scent was strong on the greyhound, but decided to keep quiet about it. For now. "Are you all right?" he barked.

The greyhound did not look directly at McKinley. "Oh, yes, fine."

"How long have you been up here?"

"A few days and nights."

"What happened?"

Duchess sat and glanced shyly at him. "You know me, McKinley, I need to run. To get about. But my human doesn't want me hanging around other dogs. Thinks I'm too highbred. So he keeps me leashed up all day—all night, too—except when *he* wants to play."

McKinley growled. "At night?"

"I'm afraid so. He stays up late watching his glow box. McKinley, I may not be the most social of dogs, but I do get lonely. And that doghouse is awful, made of foul-smelling, hard stuff. So I do what he wants. I play."

McKinley barked to show his sympathy.

"The worst of it is, every once in a while Pycraft pulls me into his truck, goes somewhere new, and makes me race against other dogs."

McKinley sighed.

"I'm fast," Duchess whined. "I know that. Actually, I enjoy racing. Besides, it's my only real chance to be with other dogs. But when I lose . . ." She looked away.

McKinley felt a rumble of anger gathering in his throat. "What happens?"

"Pycraft yells at me. Calls me dumb. Or stupid. Says it in front of other dogs, too. McKinley, I try to win, I do. But, let's face it, if I'm leashed most of the time I can't stay in shape. So, I lose. A lot. Right after I lost the last one I took off. Pycraft was so mad, he forgot to leash me right or even shut the yard entryway. It was no big deal to slip out, and . . . well, here I am."

"Not the first time."

Duchess took on a guilty look. "I suppose I should have checked with you first, but you know how it gets with us dogs and people. They need us.

And Pycraft doesn't have many friends. I get to feeling sorry for him. But, McKinley, really, I'm done with him now."

"I'm all for that," McKinley barked promptly. "But you should know something. Pycraft has put your picture up all over town."

The greyhound whimpered. "What do you mean?"

"I'm pretty sure he's trying to hunt you down."

Duchess stretched out, resting her chin on her forepaws. "McKinley, I'm not worried about people. But . . ." She looked up. "You don't think any of our pack would come after me, do you?"

"Redburn might."

Duchess came to her feet and barked.

"Don't worry. I'll assert my authority."

"Redburn does anything his people ask him to do."

"We'll see," McKinley growled. "But don't forget, I'm head dog."

The greyhound whimpered again. "Sorry for the trouble."

McKinley looked around, then leaned over. "Listen, Duchess. I heard the man in my family say there's already snow on the pass. Cold times are coming. Can you survive out here?"

She did not respond.

"Well?"

"McKinley . . . I have a new . . . friend."

"Oh?"

"She's a . . . wolf. Her name is Lupin. It was she who found me. She's amazingly strong. Hate to tell you, but I've never met anyone—among us dogs—who is so powerful. But she's kind, McKinley. And smart. You can't believe all she knows."

"Where's she coming from?"

"Up north, she told me. The Zirkel Wilderness. She's on a mission."

McKinley tried to conceal his growing worry. "What kind of mission?" He was gazing right at the greyhound.

Duchess avoided his look. "Her wolf pack has become so small, it's in danger of disappearing. She's coming to meet our pack. Get us to join the wolves up there."

McKinley growled.

"McKinley, Lupin says all dogs are descendants of wolves."

"A long time ago, yes."

"Lupin says it wasn't *that* long ago. Anyway, she believes that it's time we stopped living with people. Time to be independent again, to get back to the wild the way we once lived. That's what she said. And it's what I'm thinking of doing."

McKinley gazed at her. "Want some advice?"

"Sure."

"For the time being, stay hidden."

# 4

Among the members of McKinley's pack there were occasional arguments about wolves, debates over whether dogs were truly related to them. Some of the fancy ones, like Yophie, the Hungarian puli, or Tao, the Japanese Akita, denied it angrily, claiming they never would, or could, have anything in common with such beasts. They were purebloods, they said. Thoroughbreds.

But other dogs—usually small ones like Tubbs—rather liked the idea that they were descended from wolves.

For most of the pack, however, wolves were the subject of only idle interest.

But Duchess's news about this Lupin was very disturbing for McKinley. He considered himself a strong dog, yet to deal with a powerful wolf . . . his tail drooped at the thought.

He decided not go back to town. Instead, he spent most of the day roaming Strawberry Park, hoping to pick up some hint of the wolf's whereabouts. The last thing he needed was to be caught by surprise. He also wanted to be nearby in case Redburn showed up.

But McKinley found no trace, not a whiff. This Lupin is very clever, he thought.

It was late afternoon when McKinley returned to town. Moving briskly, alert to car traffic, he paused now and again to smell the various messages that had been left along the way. Here, Ripley had passed through. There, Hank. Montana had come from across the Yampa River. Plus a few others. All in all it was the usual mix of markings from pack members. Nothing important. McKinley hurried on. He had decided he would go right to Redburn and make sure he left Duchess alone.

He had just come in sight of Redburn's house when he heard Jack calling, "Hey, McKinley! Hey, big boy. Over here!"

McKinley stopped and looked around. The pup was on his bike at the corner.

"Come on, fella," he called again.

Noting the boy's backpack, McKinley guessed he was just getting home.

"Hey, McKinley, we're going on an adventure!" Jack cried. He slapped his leg a few times.

Understanding the gesture as one of impatience, McKinley whimpered. Here he was, on really important pack business, when his pup shows up. He would have to put off dealing with Redburn. Then again, maybe the boy just wanted to say hello.

"Come on, McKinley. Good boy! Come here!"

McKinley bounded forward. Reaching Jack, he jumped up, tail wagging.

"Way to go, McKinley!" the boy said happily. "Guess what we're going to do?"

McKinley sat down and looked up, expectant. *Going.* He knew that word.

"Mr. Pycraft lost his dog again. She's called Duchess. There are these posters up all over town. He's offering *two hundred bucks* reward to anyone who finds her!"

McKinley picked up the words *lost* and *finds,* as well as the names *Duchess* and *Pycraft.* Trying to make sense of it all, he studied the boy's excited face closely.

"McKinley," Jack went on, "do you know all the camping gear I could get with that kind of money? A one-person tent. A sleeping bag. If I decide to track that wolf—and had the right stuff—I'd really be able to stay with him."

At the words *track* and *wolf* and *stay,* McKinley barked. It was becoming clear to him that the boy was planning something to do with the wolf as well as with Pycraft. It was the word *stay* that didn't make sense. Whenever the humans said that to him, he was not supposed to move.

"So, guess what?" Jack said. "You and I are going looking for Duchess. And we're going to find her."

*Looking. Find. Duchess. Going.* This time McKinley made the connection. Jack wanted to track down Duchess. Just like the Sullivans!

Intent on keeping the boy home, McKinley stood up on his hind legs and placed his paws on the boy's shoulder. They were just about the same height.

"I knew you'd understand!" Jack cried. He gave McKinley a hug. "Come on. Let's find that dog!"

Frustrated, McKinley dropped back down, and invited the boy to play by bending down over his forepaws, opening his mouth wide, putting his tail up, and barking twice.

Jack frowned. "Come on, McKinley, I don't want to play." He checked his arm. "It's getting late. We need to give you a whiff of Duchess's scent so you can follow it."

He began to peddle away. "Come on, McKinley!" he yelled. "I need to leave my books home first."

McKinley stood his ground. Then he thought he had better go along. At least he could lead the pup away from Duchess.

With a bark, he began to follow.

"Wait here," Jack called as he brought his bike to a skidding halt in front of the house. He rushed inside.

As McKinley sat, waiting, mouth open, tongue lolling, his friend Aspen pushed through the bushes.

McKinley stood up to greet her, and the two dogs sniffed each other all over, wagging tails slowly.

Aspen detected the greyhound's scent on McKinley's coat. "Where'd you find Duchess?"

"Up in Strawberry Park. Same place she went before."

Aspen whimpered. "And I suppose you've promised to help her."

"Aspen, Duchess has been mistreated."

"I heard a rumor that Redburn will be tracking her down."

"Looks like it," McKinley growled.

Jack came bounding out of the house. McKinley looked around. In one hand the pup held some human biscuits, which he was stuffing into his mouth. In his other hand he had two large dog biscuits.

"Come on, McKinley," Jack called. "Let's go."

Aspen barked at McKinley. "Now what?"

"The pup wants to find Duchess, too."

"Are you serious?"

"Afraid so."

"But . . . why?"

"Not sure. He wants me to help him."

"Will you?"

"I'll lead him somewhere else."

"Always getting involved."

"What's that mean?"

"You watch out for everyone but yourself."

"Here you go, McKinley," Jack called, offering him a biscuit.

McKinley snapped up both.

"McKinley!" the boy cried. "You greedy cow!"

McKinley dropped one of the biscuits at Aspen's feet before swallowing the other in a gulp.

Aspen moved away without taking it up.

McKinley whined. "What's the matter?"

As the retriever retreated into the bushes she looked back over her shoulder. "When you're not so busy taking care of everyone, I'll let you know."

Disappointed, McKinley stood looking after her. Then he turned. Jack was already pedaling furiously down the way. "Come on, boy!" he was yelling.

With a sigh of frustration, McKinley loped after him.

# 5

Pycraft lived on the corner of Elk Scat Way and Raccoon Way.

Next to the house, closed off by a wire fence, was a hard-packed dirt area. In it stood two poles linked by a cable with a leash that dangled from it to the ground. Usually, Duchess was snapped onto this leash so that she could run back and forth—but little more.

There were toys scattered about, as well as rough sticks for Duchess to chew.

Next to the farther pole, and up against the rear fence, was a doghouse—like a tiny human pup's playhouse. It had a door that could be swung open. Before this door stood two dented tin food bowls.

McKinley observed it all with disgust.

"This is Mr. Pycraft's house," the pup explained as if McKinley didn't know. "I'm going to see if he'll let us into the yard so you can get a whiff of Duchess's scent. That would help you a lot, wouldn't it?"

Not sure what was about to happen, McKinley sat on the sidewalk while Jack went up to the house and knocked on the door. The boy turned to smile at him.

Feeling tense, McKinley yawned.

The house door opened, and Pycraft came out. He was a short, fat man with a sour smell about him. He also smelled of the stuff that people burned in their mouths, an odor McKinley detested.

When the man appeared, McKinley could not restrain himself from standing, wrinkling his nose, and curling his lips back from his teeth. His tail bristled.

"What do you want, kid?" the man asked. "If you're selling school junk, I'm not interested."

"Mr. Pycraft, sir, my name is Jack Kostof. I live a couple of blocks over——"

"Kostof, eh?" the man said. He was looking past the boy at McKinley. "I guess I know your dad. A tree hugger."

"Yes, sir, but I was wondering——"

"That your dog over there?"

Jack looked back over his shoulder. "McKinley? Yes, sir, that's him."

"He looks mean. He part wolf?"

"He's a malamute."

"You should keep him on a leash."

"Don't worry about McKinley, Mr. Pycraft. He's very obedient. And friendly. Wouldn't harm anyone."

The man was glaring at him. McKinley lifted his head and gave a howl of territorial claim.

"What's bugging him?" Pycraft asked.

"I don't know," Jack said.

"Kid, if you want to talk, make your dog shut up."

"McKinley!" Jack cried. "Be quiet, boy!"

McKinley suppressed the howl, but glowered at the man.

"That's better," Pycraft said. "Now, what's up, kid? I don't have all day."

"It's those posters, sir. About your missing dog."

"Oh, yeah, Duchess. I've had a few calls. Not that anyone has found her."

"I'm sure we can," Jack went on. "McKinley's a great tracker. Only I was wondering, do you have something that belongs to your dog so McKinley could sniff it? You know, so he could know Duchess's scent."

McKinley watched Pycraft glance at the pup. "Not a bad idea, kid," the man said. "You're smarter than most. Bring the dog in here." He hesitated. "But you're going to have to leash him. I don't think he likes me and I don't mess with dogs."

"I don't have a leash."

"Don't worry. I do."

"Okay."

Pycraft went into the house and closed the door behind him.

"McKinley," Jack called. "Come here, boy. Come on! I'm going to put a leash on you for just a minute."

*Leash* was a word McKinley knew, and did not like. Determined to go no nearer to that man or his house, he stood his ground.

"Come on, boy," Jack pleaded. "Good boy. Do it for me."

McKinley lowered his head, wrinkled his nose again, and flattened his ears. A growl rumbled in his chest.

The door opened, and Pycraft reappeared. In one hand was a heavy chain leash. In the other hand was a rifle. He set the gun against the wall.

McKinley growled. The few times he had been near guns when they went off had been very frightening. Partly it was the noise. But he knew well the harm they caused. Moreover, he sensed that humans were nervous about them, too. "Why'd you bring the gun?" Jack asked, alarmed.

Mr. Pycraft laughed. "Just to show that dog of

yours—if he's got any brains—not to fool with me. Now, bring him over here," he commanded.

Jack hesitated. Then he called, "McKinley. "Come on! Good boy!"

Refusing to budge, McKinley whimpered.

Jack asked for the leash. The man handed it over. Leash in hand, Jack approached McKinley. "What's the matter, boy?" he asked. "Come on. This is for me. No one's going to hurt you."

McKinley took a step back.

Pycraft snorted. "See," he snapped. "Just when you think you can control a dog, it turns on you. I know dogs, kid, and that's a nasty one you got there. Look at him, ready to attack. A dog like that, he's a menace to the whole town. I'm telling you, he's got a lot of wolf in him."

The *wolf* word, again. Whimpering, McKinley gazed at the pup's puzzled eyes, trying to make him understand the danger of this man.

"Okay, fella," Jack said softly. "I won't make you wear it." McKinley watched the boy give the leash back to Pycraft. "He won't do it, sir. I know

McKinley. Once he makes up his mind, no way I can make him."

"I could teach him," Pycraft sneered.

Jack said, "Is there something you could bring out for him to smell, something that belonged to your dog?"

"Sure," Pycraft said. "This!" He flung the leash at McKinley, who saw immediately that it would miss him. With a heavy clunk it landed at his feet.

"Dumb dog," Pycraft snapped. "I could have knocked him out silly. Serve him right."

Jack ran to the sidewalk, picked the leash up, and passed it under McKinley's nose. "Smell this, boy. Come on, McKinley," he whispered. "I really need to get that camping gear."

McKinley took a couple of loud sniffs. Duchess's smell was strong on the chain links.

"Good boy!" Jack said, and brought the leash back to Pycraft.

The man took it. "Okay, kid. Go look for Duchess, but if your dog hurts my dog, your folks are going to hear about it."

He turned and disappeared into his house, shutting the door behind him with a loud bang.

Jack came back to McKinley. "Boy, you sure don't like that guy, do you?"

McKinley, feeling more relaxed now, wagged his tail slightly.

"But you don't have to like him to find his dog, right? Come on now, McKinley, don't let me down. Find Duchess!"

# 6

McKinley gazed up at Jack, whined, and lifted his paw.

The boy squatted down before him. "You know Duchess's smell now, big guy," he said. "I know you do. So come on, put your nose to the ground and find her. For me, okay?"

McKinley lay down, resting his head on his forepaws. Strawberry Park was the one place he would not go.

"Don't quit on me, McKinley," Jack pleaded. "*Please.* I really want to find her. Come on, boy. Let's find Duchess!"

Rolling his eyes, McKinley studied Jack. Why, he wondered, couldn't humans spend as much time learning about dogs as dogs spent on humans? He needed to tire the pup out so he would give up the search on his own. Then he remembered the perfect place, a trail that headed straight into the woods at the end of Horse Smell Way. Trees and bushes grew thickly on both sides. On one side a small creek trickled—Fish Creek, the dogs called it. Most of all, the trail was a stiff climb.

McKinley rose to his feet and gave himself a shake. He looked at the sky. Night was not far off. He should be able to exhaust the boy before dark. With a sharp bark, McKinley broke into a run.

"Hey!" Jack jumped on his bike and pedaled hard to catch up.

With a look back at the pup, McKinley ran on, his nose to the ground as if he were following a scent. All the while he wagged his tail so the boy would think they were on a real hunt.

"Way to go, boy! You can find her!" Jack cried,

pedaling furiously. "I bet she's close, huh? Good boy!"

After a short distance the trail narrowed and rose so steeply that Jack had to stop and dismount from his bike. Running, he pushed it to the top of the hill.

McKinley was waiting for him.

"Did Duchess come this way, fella?" Jack called. "How long ago? I'm getting tired."

Barking twice, McKinley dropped into his playful posture, inviting Jack to roughhouse.

"Stop, McKinley," Jack snapped. "No fooling around. I really want that reward money. Keep going."

*Stop. Going.* McKinley understood. He halted his frisking, looked around, and watched the treetops sway. There was usually a breeze before the darkness came.

Two trails led away from the hilltop. One was easy for the bike. The other wound upward into the foothills. Determined to make the pup want to quit, McKinley bolted for the high trail, tail wagging, mouth open.

Jack, pedaling again, followed after. In a few moments he stopped. "McKinley!" he shouted. "Hold on. This is too steep for me!" He dumped his bike to the ground and began to run.

McKinley barked and continued on. Once, twice, he looked back. Jack was puffing hard.

"McKinley," the pup called. "Not so fast!"

Each time Jack caught up, McKinley bounded off. By the time they reached the top of the next hill, the pup was thoroughly winded.

"Think . . . we have . . . a lot farther . . . to go?" he panted.

McKinley barked again and ran ahead.

"Come on!" Jack begged. "Slow down!"

They came to a level area, and McKinley went on at a slower pace.

"Better," the boy said.

But then once again the trail rose. It became narrower, crowded in by rough, often sharp rocks.

"How much . . . time till . . . we . . . get to Duchess?" Jack asked when he caught up, even more bushed than before.

McKinley pawed the ground, barked sharply, and went forward a few paces.

"Wait!" Jack commanded. He threw himself down and leaned against a rock. "I need to rest for a moment, boy."

Glad to oblige, McKinley came back, sank down, and lowered his head to Jack's leg. When the boy fondled his ears, he thumped the ground with his tail.

"This is pretty much a canyon, isn't it?" Jack said, looking up and down the trail. "Perfect place for an ambush," he added. "Wonder if in the old days it ever happened."

McKinley, not understanding any of these words, closed his eyes. The sky was darkening. They would have to be turning back soon. It was the perfect moment for the boy to give up.

"Tell you what," the pup said. "If we don't find that stupid Duchess soon, we're heading home. Come back tomorrow. Earlier. Okay?"

Hearing the word *home*, McKinley wagged his tail.

Jack stood up. "Come on, big boy," he said. "A

little more. If I get that reward I'll buy you a juicy hamburger all for yourself."

McKinley came to his feet slowly, then continued along the now-narrow trail. Suddenly, he halted and sniffed. A growl rose in his throat.

"What's up, McKinley?" Jack called. "Did you smell Duchess? Did you find her? Come on, keep going!"

McKinley stared ahead. It was the wolf. Not only was she on the trail before them, she was coming in their direction.

# 7

"McKinley?" the boy asked, "is something the matter?"

McKinley stood stiff-legged, body leaning forward, ears pricked up, nose wrinkled and lips pulled back to expose his teeth. His tail bristled and the black hair rose along the ridge on his back.

With McKinley's instincts urging him to flee, he darted a look back over his shoulder to see if a retreat was clear. It was. But the pup was behind him. And he knew he must protect Jack.

As the wolf's scent grew stronger, it took all of McKinley's courage not to shrink away. He forced himself—body trembling—to move forward, shielding the boy from the approaching danger.

From around the bend in the trail, Lupin limped into Jack's view.

"McKinley!" the pup gasped. "It's the wolf!"

As big as McKinley was, Lupin was bigger. Broad shouldered with a massive head, she had bright, piercing eyes and powerful jaws. Her legs were strong, her paws huge, larger than McKinley's.

The wolf continued to approach until she was within an easy leap of McKinley. There she halted, her crooked foot raised, her head high, ears pointing almost straight up. Her glowing eyes were focused right on McKinley. From her throat emerged a low rumble: "They call me Lupin."

McKinley tried to return the wolf's stare but was overwhelmed with a sense of his own weakness. Unable to hide his fear, he backed up a step and lowered his body. His ears flattened. His tail drooped. "I'm called McKinley," he whimpered.

"You are a dog."

"I am . . . yes."

"Dog," the wolf growled, "you who live with humans, who take food from their hands and garbage piles, do you know who your ancestors were? Do you know your true family and what kind of blood runs even now through your veins?"

"The blood of . . . wolves," McKinley whined softly.

"Yes, *wolves*. The free ones," Lupin snapped. "Yet you choose to be no more than a groveling servant to humans."

McKinley tried to stand taller. "I am head dog."

"Head dog over whom?" Lupin barked. "Over a pack of weak-legged, tongue-lapping, tail-wagging slaves who take their food from bowls! Have you no honor, McKinley? No pride?

"You call yourself head dog," Lupin growled, "but are you a true leader? Is not that feeble pup behind you your real master?" Lupin shook her head, causing her thick mane to ripple. "Look at you! Collar-wearer. Leash-licker. Shake your head and you will hear the tinkle of tags that say you belong to—that you are *owned* by—some human.

I dare you to look at your reflection in a stream. You will see the wolf in you.

"McKinley, if you were true to your nature, you could still be a wolf. Imagine what it would be like to live in the wilderness with a pack of free wolves. Sense how it would be to match your wits and strength with the best. Consider the courage it takes to live and die through the use of your own muscles and intelligence. Think what it means to have whelps who are born free—who can never be taken from you.

"McKinley, our meeting here today is no accident. I tracked you down so that you might hear my message. You are easy to find. You stink of human food."

McKinley hung his head.

"You call yourself head dog, but with one stroke of my crooked paw, I could send you tumbling into the mud. Beware of me, McKinley, for I am a free wolf!"

McKinley quailed. He could not help himself. His ears fell back. He stuck out his tongue in submission.

Suddenly, Lupin leaped forward. Landing close to McKinley, she held her head higher than ever, sharp teeth exposed.

McKinley, collapsing in terror, rolled over and, with his paws limp, exposed his belly.

"So much for you, dog!" Lupin barked. Then she lifted her nose to the sky, shaped her mouth into an almost perfect circle, and let forth a howl. It was part moan, part cry of triumph, throaty and rough-edged at first, then rising to a single clear note that vaulted high and echoed down the canyon.

The sound terrified McKinley. Engulfed him. He was sure he was about to be attacked.

Except the wolf backed away and only growled, "I did not come to humiliate you, McKinley. Stand up."

Obedient, McKinley rolled over, rose, and stole a look at Lupin. The wolf had relaxed. Her tail—no longer bristling—wagged gently. Her mouth was open. McKinley could see her tongue.

"I did not want to make you submit," Lupin

whined. "I only wished to make you understand what you've become."

McKinley lowered his head. "I understood."

"Listen to me, dog. Duchess has become my friend. She told me of you. She admires you. I know all about your pack, too. You are a good leader, strong and caring. You are worthy of the position and name 'head dog.'"

McKinley sighed. "Thank you."

"But, dog, you remain a slave to humans. So I urge you, return to the wilderness. Join my pack. Hunted by men with guns and traps, we are diminishing rapidly. We need dogs like you to replenish us."

McKinley stole a glance to where Jack stood a few feet behind, staring wide-eyed at the wolf.

Lupin noticed the look. "The pup may even be a good human, McKinley. But he remains human, so full of fear and submission, he will turn himself into a cruel master. What I offer you and your pack is a life of freedom."

That said, she began to move away.

Just before taking the turn in the trail, Lupin stopped and looked back over her massive shoulder. "I will not be far, McKinley. I can find you whenever I wish. Think about what I have said. Better yet, act on it. You are a head dog now, McKinley. But you could become a great dog. You could lead your whole pack to their liberation."

McKinley, watching the wolf disappear from view, stood very still.

# 8

In all his life McKinley had never met so awesome an animal as Lupin. Far from feeling ashamed of his submissive behavior, he felt stronger. It was as if he were linked now to some invincible force.

"McKinley!" Jack's voice startled him. "Is he really gone?"

The pup was standing a few yards back along the trail, the smell of fear strong on him.

Excited, McKinley bounded over. He dropped down on his front paws. His tail went up. He barked.

"Are you crazy, McKinley?" Jack cried. "Don't you have any idea who that was?"

McKinley sat back and studied Jack intently. The pup seemed small, weak.

"McKinley," he said in a hushed voice, "that was the wolf."

The boy went down on his knees.

"Wasn't he wonderful?" He threw his arms around McKinley's neck and buried his face in his dog's fur. "And you were great."

Puzzled, McKinley wagged his tail.

"McKinley," the boy went on, "I'm sure that's the wolf I saw before. Wasn't he beautiful? And powerful. In that story, *The Jungle Book,* this kid lives with wolves just like that. They teach him all this neat stuff. That would be so cool."

The boy glanced at the sky. It had darkened. The moon had risen behind clouds. He said, "We better get going. The folks will be worried if I'm not home soon." He grasped McKinley's collar. "Home, boy," he said. "Take us home."

McKinley, barking twice at the word *home,* began moving back down the trail.

Jack continued to chatter as they traveled. "I did

see a lot of wolves once, at the zoo in Denver. But you know what, McKinley? They didn't look so great. I mean, this one is so cool, isn't he? But did you notice his limp? Wonder what happened to him, where he came from. I mean, if I joined up with him I wouldn't have to stay with the wolves long. Just a week, maybe. Be so sweet. Double sweet.

"Thing is, I bet my parents wouldn't let me. They'd say, like, I'm too young. Or, you know, I can't miss school. So I'd have to do it without them knowing."

Paying little attention to Jack, McKinley was still enthralled by the sense of power that had radiated from Lupin. And her challenge. It was troubling.

Something about what he'd heard made him uneasy. He had always considered himself completely free. True, from time to time there had been problems: made to stay in the house when he hadn't wished to; the occasional questioning of his authority as the town's head dog; the difficulties humans—such as Pycraft—presented. But, all in all, he had always believed he lived a good life. Yet Lupin was freer than him.

The more McKinley thought about that, the more he found Jack's grip on his collar irritating, as if he were being choked.

Shaking his head vigorously, he forced the boy to let go.

"Sorry, boy," Jack said. "Didn't mean to hurt you."

For a moment, McKinley recalled the wolf's scent. It was free of anything human. Just the thought of it made McKinley pant with amazement.

"Hey, McKinley, do you think you can find my bike?" he heard Jack say as though from a distant place.

McKinley looked around. The boy's face, in the cloud-shrouded moonlight, seemed soft, helpless.

"We never did find Duchess, did we, McKinley?" the pup said. "But you know what? It doesn't matter. I'm not going to tell my folks I saw the wolf again. Even Dad said I shouldn't talk about him. He thinks people would hunt any wolf down. And if I'm going after him——"

McKinley growled.

Jack said, "What's the matter?"

Having heard the words *hunt* and *wolf,* McKinley gazed at the boy, head cocked.

"Hey," Jack said, "if I went off to join the wolves, would you come with me? You understand, don't you, boy?" Speaking slowly, the pup pointed to himself. "*I'm* going to *stay* with"——he pointed back up the trail——"the wolves."

At last McKinley understood: Jack wanted to go off with Lupin. The idea horrified him. Fine for Duchess, but not the boy. Duchess could survive. Jack would not.

He turned and trotted off, not stopping till they reached the pup's bike.

"Good boy," Jack cried when he saw it. He bent over and tried to give McKinley another hug.

McKinley backed away.

"Hey, don't act so insulted, McKinley. It'll be all right, I promise. I won't stay with the wolf forever.

Anyway, I told you, if you want, you can come with me."

Furious at the boy for even considering such a thing, McKinley turned his back on him and began to trot off.

Jack leaped on his bike and began to pedal. "Hey, boy, don't go so fast. I know you want to get home. But it's too dark for me to see."

McKinley ran, forcing Jack to pump as hard as he could just to keep up.

**9**

When they reached home, Jack went right inside. McKinley hung back. He wanted to find Aspen and tell her everything that had happened.

He trotted over to the bushes that separated the two houses and pushed his way through. When he came out on the other side, he barked once, twice.

There was no response.

Disappointed, McKinley retreated. Opening the door to Jack's house by his usual method, he went inside. Sarah, the pup's mother, was in the food place.

"Hi, McKinley, old boy," she said, greeting him

warmly. "That was so clever, Jack teaching you to open doors."

McKinley paused to look at her. She was a tall human, always smelling of interesting food. "He's in his room," she said. "Our dinner will be ready soon. Better get him to feed you."

McKinley went to Jack's room. The boy was propped up on his soft sleeping place, gazing again at a block of staring papers.

"Look here," Jack whispered to McKinley, pointing. "Exactly what that wolf was like."

Instead of looking, McKinley studied the boy. How was he going to keep the pup from running off?

"McKinley," the boy confided, "they're so cool, aren't they? Think you want to come with me?"

Whimpering, McKinley let his tail droop.

"That's okay, pal," Jack said. "I can go on my own." He got up and slid open his clothing box door. On the floor was a jumble of shoes, balls, a skateboard, a snow-sliding board. From the bottom the boy pulled out his new backpack, the one with the extra straps. McKinley recognized it as something Jack had taken with him when they slept in the woods during the hot time.

"Best birthday gift I ever got," the pup said. "I better start pulling my gear together." He looked over to McKinley. "Now don't go telling my folks."

The dog barked with frustration.

"McKinley, shhh! I know what I'm doing."

Turning, McKinley went outside and sniffed the air for Aspen. He wanted her to know about the wolf—and about the boy. When he discovered that she was still not around, he lay down with a sigh. Maybe Aspen was right. Life was getting too complicated. He had to take care of Duchess. And Jack. And if the pup ran off . . . but Lupin had come for dogs, not for humans.

Smelling dinner, he went back into the house. McKinley gazed at the woman, wishing there was some way he could tell her what the pup was planning.

"McKinley," she said, "how many times have I told you, if you're hungry, tell Jack to get your dinner. That's his job."

McKinley contented himself with some water.

While the humans ate, he listened closely. The boy said nothing about the wolf. Instead, he used other words, which McKinley did not know. From time to time Jack looked at him and gave a wink. A glum McKinley gazed at him, whimpering twice. At one point, wanting the boy to tell Sarah and Gil about what he was planning, he put a paw on the pup's arm.

"What's bothering McKinley?" the woman asked.

"Beats me," Jack said, bending over his food.

Gil said, "I think you forgot to feed him."

Jack started up. "Dang! Sorry, McKinley!" He hurried to fill McKinley's bowl, placing three biscuits on top of the food.

After eating, a discouraged McKinley went outside again. The night air was thick with the aroma of human dinners. Redburn had come by. Only a few dogs were out now, none needing his attention. A block away a skunk passed by in search of garbage. Cats were prowling through the darkness.

Finally, Aspen appeared, mouth slightly open,

tail wagging. McKinley stood, and the dogs sniffed each other, then sat side by side.

Aspen lifted one paw in mild apprehension. "What's that smell on you? I can't place it."

"A wolf."

Aspen immediately stood and barked. "Tell me."

McKinley recounted his meeting with Lupin. "She was . . . amazing. And she isn't just passing through. She told Duchess her pack is dying out. She's trying to get the dogs from around here to join it."

Aspen was staring at him with intense interest. "Did you really submit to her?" She sat again, to listen.

"I didn't have much choice."

"Would you . . . want to follow her?"

McKinley looked away. "Don't know that, either. I'm head dog—unless Lupin comes here to challenge me. Or until some other dog hears about what happened and makes a challenge. And I lose."

"McKinley, ease up. Think about what *you* want."

McKinley whimpered. "I know. . . ." He stretched out on the ground, his head on his forepaws.

Aspen gave him a lick across his nose. "You worry too much."

McKinley beat his tail on the ground. "I just hope the humans don't learn about Lupin."

"Will Jack tell?"

"When the family ate, he never said the *wolf* word."

This time it was Aspen who whimpered.

"And guess what?" McKinley glanced toward his house. "I'm pretty sure my human pup wants to run off with Lupin."

"You're kidding."

McKinley sighed. "Wish I were. It's crazy. I have to help Duchess get away. I have to make sure the boy stays. I have to deal with the wolf."

"McKinley," Aspen growled, "Redburn was here."

"I smelled him. What did he want?"

"Said he had something to tell you."

Yawning nervously, McKinley stood up and shook himself. Then he lifted his head and gave a drawn-out howl to let the neighborhood know he was ready to defend his territory. Even as he called out, Lupin's howl reverberated in his head. Her howl was bolder, stronger. He wished he could howl like that.

Aspen remained still.

McKinley turned to her. "Guess I better go find Redburn."

"I'll be around."

With a slow wag of his tail, McKinley started off, trotting through the quiet ways, claws clicking on the pavement. Occasionally a car passed by. Few humans were out. From time to time McKinley looked through house windows into rooms where he saw people watching their glow boxes or holding staring papers in their hands. He could see dogs asleep on rugs, on couches. All was calm. Peaceful.

It is a good life here, McKinley thought, as if he were having an argument with himself. Then he recalled Lupin's description of a wolf's life, wondering: Which is better? This or that?

When McKinley reached Redburn's house on

Pine Smell Way, he peered through the white picket fence. Seeing lights on, he barked twice.

Within moments the front door opened. McKinley saw a human behind it, but it was Redburn who came out and loped down the path.

Even at night the setter's fur seemed burnished. When he drew close to McKinley, he stopped and tossed his head.

McKinley chose to take his stand in a power position, stiff-legged, tail raised, ears forward. He barked once, then again. "You came by my place."

Redburn growled. "Thought I'd let you know my human and I are going to track down Duchess tomorrow morning. She's up by the Strawberry Park boulders. Isn't she?"

"What makes you so sure?"

Redburn snorted. "Everyone knows that's where she goes. I'll lead my human right there."

McKinley wrinkled his nose. "Don't."

"Why not?

"Duchess has every right to run away. She was being mistreated."

"Nothing to do with me."

McKinley issued a soft, low-pitched growl. "Of course it does. Would you want to be leashed all the time? Locked up in a yard? Kept in a doghouse hardly big enough for a rabbit?"

"McKinley, when are you going to understand? The power in Steamboat Springs is with humans, not dogs. It's smarter to do what humans want you to do. Makes life easier."

"Leash-licker!" McKinley snapped—Lupin's insult, he realized.

Head high, Redburn glared at him. Then he turned and began to trot away.

McKinley barked. "Do you have to do *everything* your master tells you to do?"

Redburn stopped and looked back. "At least I don't have a pup giving me orders. McKinley, if anyone should be head dog around here, it's me."

McKinley growled. "I'm going to stop you tomorrow."

When Redburn reached the door of his house, he scratched to be let in. As the door opened, he glanced back at McKinley. "Don't try it," he snapped. "You'll only regret it."

McKinley watched the setter disappear into the house. That dumb dog, he thought, is going to lead his human to Duchess. But what they'll find is Lupin.

# 10

Next morning McKinley was awake the minute the bell box in Jack's room began to ring. He jumped off the soft sleeping place—where he, too, had slept—and gazed at the still-sleeping pup.

"How am I going to keep him from going off with Lupin?" McKinley asked himself again. Having no answer, and knowing this was a gathering day with other pups, he thrust his wet nose into Jack's face and began to lick.

The boy responded by turning over, hitting the bell box, then drawing his coverings over his head.

"Go away, you dumb dog," he murmured. "I want to sleep."

McKinley barked. The barking drew the female to the room.

"Hey, Jack," she called in her big voice. "Let's go, guy. McKinley is right. Check your clock. Time for school."

McKinley joined in with more loud barking.

"I'm tired," the boy groaned, burrowing deeper under his coverings. "Do I have to go to school?"

McKinley took hold of the boy's coverings with his teeth and pulled.

"McKinley," the boy screamed. "Stop!" He sat up and worked the sleep out of his eyes.

"Thataway," Sarah said. "Now take your shower and get dressed." She left the room.

A grumpy Jack remained sitting on the edge of his sleeping place.

McKinley wagged his tail, lifted himself up with his front paws, and barked into the boy's face.

"Why'd you have to call her?" Jack said, using two hands to shove him down. "I could have slept five more minutes. Go away!"

McKinley, tail drooping, went to the kitchen. The female was working on the boy's food. The male sat at the sitting board looking over a pile of staring papers while drinking something steamy.

"Morning, McKinley," he mumbled.

McKinley checked his food bowl, only to find it empty. Annoyed, he put his paw into it and flipped it over, making a clatter. When that had no effect, he did the same with his empty water bowl.

The man put aside his staring papers and stood up. "Okay, McKinley, I get the message. I'm coming."

McKinley wagged his tail and barked his appreciation.

"This is supposed to be Jack's job," the man grumbled good-naturedly.

As soon as the bowls were filled, McKinley swallowed his food, lapped up some water, then hurried to the door.

Gripping the doorknob in his mouth, he twisted and pulled the door open a bit, then used his nose to open it wider. He was just about to head out when the boy ran up. "Hey, McKinley," he called.

McKinley looked around.

Jack said, "Just because Dad taught you to open doors doesn't mean you're on your own. Come to school with me."

McKinley, head cocked, considered the boy. First he's angry at me. Then he wants to play. Annoyed, McKinley went outside.

"Don't go far!" Jack shouted after him.

The air was cooler and damper than before. Foggy in the mountains. McKinley understood what that meant: Snow would be coming soon.

He lifted his nose and took in the smells. A whiff of cooking meat came from some houses. Cats were on their morning prowls. It was the day loud trucks came for the food people wished to share.

McKinley padded to the end of the driveway to check if any messages had been left for him. Aspen, he noted, was out and long gone.

With a sigh, McKinley trotted to the middle of the way and looked up and down. The neighborhood was as calm as usual. People were starting from their homes. A few pups were already heading for their daily gathering.

McKinley peered back over his shoulder at Jack's house. He knew the boy wanted him to come along. But it was Duchess who was mostly in McKinley's mind. Human hunters were early risers. There was a good likelihood that the male Sullivan had already gone off, taking Redburn with him.

Giving a low moan of impatience, McKinley took off with a quick bound. Jack would have to get to his gathering place without him. After all, he had called him dumb. He could almost hear what Lupin would make of that. Just thinking of it made McKinley tense.

Halfway to Redburn's house, McKinley heard a bark. He stopped and peered around. Tubbs, the basset hound, squirmed out from under some bushes, tail wagging.

"Morning, McKinley!"

He stood still while Tubbs trotted over. "Hey, McKinley, guess what?"

"What?"

"There's this rumor going around town about a wolf coming down from the hills."

McKinley gazed at him. "No kidding?"

"It's true. Ollie, from over on Garlic Smell Way, told me."

"Did Ollie see the wolf himself?"

"No."

"Hey, Tubbs, don't believe everything you hear." With one wag of his tail, McKinley hurried away.

The rumor worried him. News about Lupin would move fast. By dinnertime the whole dog pack would know about her. And they would turn to him to know what to do.

But McKinley had no answers. Not about anything.

He reached Redburn's house the moment the front door opened and the setter loped into the yard. The male Sullivan followed. They were heading for a truck.

Seeing McKinley, Redburn lifted a bristling tail and barked vigorously.

McKinley ignored him, but he was thinking.

Redburn could not track Duchess from a truck. He would have to start from Pycraft's house. Yes, that was where they were probably going.

With an impulsive, angry bark, McKinley wheeled about and galloped away toward Horse Smell Way. This was no time for questions that had no answers. The best, and easiest, thing to do was to get to Duchess first and help her get away.

# 11

Long and looping, Horse Smell Way led over a high ridge, sweeping in and around a part of town crowded with new houses. Usually the way provided a fine view of the mountains but the morning's fog made it hard to see.

Moving at a steady trot, McKinley kept to the side of the way, not wanting to be surprised by car, bicycle, or human runner.

As he crested the top of the ridge, he heard barking. Pausing, he peered into the fog and sniffed. It was Nemo, a wiry spaniel whose house stood some distance from the others'. Nemo's humans did not like him playing with the rest of the pack.

Nemo stood in the middle of the way, holding to a respectful stance. McKinley, as head dog, paused, allowing himself to be sniffed.

"How come you're up here?" Nemo wanted to know once formal greetings were complete.

"Heading for Strawberry Park."

Nemo's ears pricked up with interest. "Hey, do you want some company?" He stole an anxious look at his own house. "It's early," Nemo whined. "My humans sleep late. I bet I could get away."

"Thanks, no."

"Hey," Nemo yapped, "I heard some gossip that there's a wolf up there. Is that what you're doing, looking for him?"

"I don't think so." McKinley set off without glancing back.

Nemo scampered after him. "Hey, McKinley, I think I know where an old fox——"

McKinley stopped abruptly, turned, planted his feet, wrinkled his nose, and growled.

Nemo skidded to a halt. He dropped his tail between his legs and sighed. "Sorry, I didn't mean to be pushy. . . ." He slunk away.

McKinley trotted on, mouth open, ears forward. But he was worried. If a dog like Nemo knew about Lupin, the rest of the pack dogs must know. Had they heard about the wolf's challenge? No, he thought, only Aspen knows.

As McKinley came off the ridge, the fog thinned enough so that he could see down the hill to the pups' gathering place. They were arriving in bunches by car and bicycle. Dogs played around them. A lot of the young humans were running about, tossing pointed balls.

McKinley hated those balls. No matter how much he stretched his mouth, they were impossible to grip. A *baseball*—one of Jack's favorite words—was so much more fun to play with.

"Kids!" a voice called from below. "Almost time for school. Start putting games away."

Just then McKinley saw Jack—on his bicycle—race into the car place. Within seconds the pup was surrounded by others his size. McKinley wondered if he was telling them about the wolf.

The next moment he saw Jack chasing after another pup with a pointed ball, leap at him, and knock him down. He's good at that, McKinley thought.

As he kept on, a couple of dogs looked up at him. One—his name was Montana—barked a greeting. Then another—Lily—spied him, too, and began to yap. "Hey, McKinley, is it true about the wolf?"

McKinley could not stop. Duchess needed him.

He soon reached the small house in Strawberry Park. It appeared as abandoned as ever.

McKinley checked the aspen tree in front of the house to see if there were any new messages. All he found was Duchess's scent. He left a mark just in case anyone was looking for him.

Nervous now, McKinley gazed at the woods beyond the field. With the white fog seeping through them, the pines and aspen groves seemed to be drifting. He scratched himself behind one ear. He was stalling and he knew it.

McKinley lifted his head and sniffed the air. A slight breeze rippled in from the north but bore no hint of either Duchess or Lupin. Perhaps they were gone. That would be good. He could easily take care of Redburn.

He sniffed again. The weather was changing.

McKinley was still pondering what to do when he caught the sound of human voices. People were coming down Fox Haven Way. Though he could neither smell nor see who it was, every instinct told him it was Sullivan and Redburn. And Pycraft. There was little choice: He had to act as if Duchess was still up in the boulders.

Repressing a bark, he bounded across the way that ran before the little house, sprinted over the field, and plunged up into the woods. As soon as he was under cover he halted and looked back. Sure enough, Redburn, his nose down, tail wagging, was sniffing his way toward the house. Sullivan was right there with him. Walking a short way behind was Pycraft, his rifle in his hands. It was as long and thin as he was short and fat.

Seeing the gun, McKinley wrinkled his nose and growled with anger. Were they going to shoot Duchess?

As the humans talked, McKinley kept his eyes on Redburn. It took only seconds before the setter discovered McKinley's fresh mark.

Redburn looked across the field to the woods and began to bark.

Sullivan turned. "What's the matter, fella?" McKinley heard him say. "Smell something?"

Redburn yelped a few times, informing him about McKinley. Sullivan, not understanding, patted the dog on the head, then beckoned Pycraft over. Pycraft pulled something out of a jacket pocket. McKinley recognized it as the leash that had been thrown at him. The man shoved it into Redburn's face so the setter could smell Duchess's scent.

Sullivan cried loudly, "Okay, Redburn, you got us this far. Now find Duchess. Come on, fella! Find her!"

Redburn, whimpering, swung around to face the woods.

McKinley could almost see the glint in his eyes but he could not know his thoughts: Redburn had his master's commands—telling him to go forward after Duchess—ringing in his ears. He also knew that McKinley was in the woods, waiting for him. The question was, what would Redburn do?

# 12

"Come on, Redburn," Sullivan insisted. "Go find Duchess! Do it for me, boy."

As McKinley looked on, Redburn lowered his tail and began to bark loudly. "Keep out of my way, McKinley!"

"Shut that fool dog up!" Pycraft snapped. "If Duchess is out there, she'll get scared away."

Sullivan, frowning, stepped forward and patted Redburn on the head again. "Easy, boy," he said. "Just do your thing, big fella. Find Duchess. You'll get a special treat when you do. Get back on the trail now."

Redburn licked the man's hands. Then he raised his tail and allowed himself a low growl. "McKinley, I know you're out there."

"Maybe my gun is scaring him," Pycraft said. "But like I warned you, there might be snakes up in those woods. I don't want to mess with them. Give me the willies."

"Don't worry," Sullivan assured him. "Seeing the gun lets him know we're on a hunt. That's the way I trained him."

"He's sure looking skittish," Pycraft said.

McKinley, observing the whole scene, felt disgust.

"Give me the gun," Sullivan said. Pycraft handed it over. "Come on, fella," Sullivan urged, waving the gun in front of the setter's face. "Hunting time."

With a snort, Redburn crossed the way, then pranced nervously into the field.

"That-a-boy," Sullivan said.

McKinley, looking on, realized suddenly that Redburn was following *his* scent. Well, then, he would lead Redburn in the wrong direction, leaving a trail that would lure the setter and the humans away from the boulders—and away from Duchess.

Not caring if he made any noise, McKinley plunged through the woods. As he went, he brushed up against trees and bushes so his trail would be strong. He was so sure about his trick, he did not even look back.

He soon reached a place where the foliage was as thick as a wall. And the fog was dense again, too, blanketing all smells.

Panting, McKinley paused, looked back, and listened intently. He could see nothing of Redburn. Nor could he hear anything from the humans.

Puzzled by the silence, McKinley edged back the way he had come. Every few steps he halted, lifting his head to listen and sniff.

Only when he had retraced half of his own trail did he hear sounds. Voices. But they were moving *away*.

It was then that McKinley knew it was he who had been fooled. Redburn and the humans were not following his scent, but the one Duchess had left. And they were heading straight for the boulders.

Furious with himself, McKinley charged back, crashing through the woods, thinking he would head them off. He was going so fast, he tripped. Tumbling head over heels, he crashed into a stump. Stunned, he stood up on wobbly legs, shook his head clear, and looked around.

He had come to an area of dense woods. The thick foggy air almost dripped. He listened hard.

"The dog must be in there," he heard Sullivan say.

It was only a whisper, but enough to make McKinley realize he'd come down too far. Heart thumping, he crept back through the thick foliage. Gradually, he began to pick up the scent. The two men, as well as Redburn, were between him and the boulders.

McKinley decided to hold back, then startle them so Duchess could escape. For the greatest surprise he would come at them from behind.

He lifted his nose to catch the direction of the wind. Not that the humans could detect his approach, but Redburn would. Being downwind of the setter would help conceal him. Crawling, McKinley stole forward.

"Bet you anything Duchess is right in among those boulders," Pycraft said. "Come on, Duchess, you stupid dog. Get on out. You hear me?"

Drawing closer, McKinley sighted the boulders. Pycraft was standing on one side of the open space, Duchess's leash in hand. Sullivan was on the other side, holding the long gun. Between the two was Redburn. The setter had his tail stuck straight behind him, one paw lifted, head extended forward. He was pointing right at the boulders.

"Keep the rifle handy," Pycraft warned. "Remember what I told you about snakes. If they're going to be anywhere, it'll be by those rocks."

"Don't worry," Sullivan said. "I'm ready."

"Come on, Duchess," Pycraft crooned.

To McKinley it was a sickening sound.

"Time to get on home, baby. Got some good food for you, girl." Pycraft stretched his other hand out. There was a dog biscuit in it.

McKinley, watching intently, was not sure when

to rush forward. Perhaps Duchess would not stir and there would be no need. Surely the greyhound knew that the men were there, and that they could not go in after her.

Suddenly Redburn cringed, lowered himself, and let out a high-pitched whine. He looked around at Sullivan.

"What's the matter with him?" Pycraft cried.

"I don't know."

McKinley knew immediately. The dog must have detected Lupin's presence. But was it just the wolf's scent, or was she actually close?

Pycraft was edging forward. "I know you're in there, Duchess sweetie," he coaxed. "Come on, baby. Come to Papa."

Duchess poked her face out of the entry hole. Her big eyes shifted from Pycraft to Redburn, then to Sullivan. When she saw the long gun, she cowered and whimpered.

Pycraft moved closer. Squatting, he stretched out the hand holding the biscuit. He kept the leash in his other hand, behind his back.

McKinley was sure Duchess would know about the leash. Why was she still moving forward?

"Here you go, girl," Pycraft coaxed, showing the biscuit. "You got to be hungry. I know you are. Here. It's your favorite kind. Bacon flavored."

Duchess, you fool! McKinley worried. What are you doing? Get back into the boulders!

But Duchess, tail tucked low, continued to slink from her hiding place. Now she was in the open. McKinley heard her whimper, and saw her look anxiously at Sullivan.

"That-a-girl," Pycraft kept saying. He dropped the leash to the ground and reached out toward his dog. Duchess, her body low, crept toward him.

Redburn, meanwhile, was edging away. One paw was partly raised, his tongue was out, his tail down but wagging slightly.

Sullivan turned to his dog. "What's the matter, big boy?" he demanded. "You did your job. What's getting at you?"

McKinley was now sure that Lupin was nearby and drawing closer. But from what direction?

Pycraft was just about to grab Duchess when a gray blur exploded from the boulder entryway. The instant the wolf hit the ground, she rushed at Pycraft. The human went sprawling onto his back, arms spread wide.

Lupin, mouth wide, teeth exposed, straddled him, snarling. "Leave Duchess alone!" she barked.

An astonished McKinley just stared.

"Help! Help!" Pycraft screamed. "Get him off of me!"

Redburn, far from helping, skittered away, tail tucked between his legs.

Sullivan raised the long gun and aimed it right at Lupin.

At that moment McKinley reared up from the bushes where he had been hiding, tore into the clearing, and leaped at Sullivan. Even as he struck the man, the gun fired.

McKinley heard a high-pitched yelp from Lupin as she rolled away from Pycraft's body.

Sullivan, reeling from the impact of McKinley's forepaws, fell to his knees, dropping the gun.

McKinley whirled. "Duchess!" he barked. "Lupin! Run!"

The greyhound, terrified, seemed to be standing on her toes. McKinley clamped his teeth onto the gun. At the same time a bleeding Lupin struggled to her feet and bolted behind the boulders.

Pycraft lunged forward on his knees, grabbing hold of Duchess by a rear leg. Yapping with pain, the greyhound tried to pull free.

"It's a wolf!" Pycraft cried, holding fast to Duchess. "Get him, Sullivan! Get the wolf!"

Sullivan snatched at the gun, but McKinley, snarling and growling, hung on fiercely.

With a yank, Sullivan pulled the gun from McKinley's teeth and ran behind the rocks. He was shouting, "Redburn! Get after him, boy. Go!"

Following his master's orders, a frightened Redburn began to creep forward.

McKinley jumped at the setter, knocking him down. Then he thrust his snout close to one of the dog's silky ears. "Go after that wolf and you'll never get back home!"

Redburn, eyes rolled up, did not move.

"Get the wolf!" Pycraft screamed. "Get him!" He held Duchess tightly with two arms now.

McKinley heard two shots from the boulders. With a frightened howl, he spun about and plunged down the hill as fast as he could run.

# 13

By the time McKinley let himself into his house he was no longer afraid, just exhausted. And his mouth hurt from clamping onto Pycraft's gun.

He sniffed the air. No one was home. Relieved, he returned to the front yard and flopped down. Still panting, he gave himself over to worry.

He had failed miserably. Duchess had been captured by Pycraft. Lupin had been wounded. And there were those extra, frightening shots from Sullivan. For all he knew, the wolf had been killed. And for what reason? Because Duchess wanted to be free. McKinley sighed. If

Lupin was hurt—or killed—was it his fault? Oh, why did humans think they owned dogs?

The thought was very painful. If Lupin was alive, perhaps he should run off with her to the wilderness. He closed his eyes and tried to imagine what it would be like. Visions of dark woods, cold nights, and sleeting snow filled his mind.

He had barely begun to doze when he heard a bark. "McKinley, what happened?"

He lifted his head. Aspen was standing close by, ears pitched forward, tail wagging slowly.

McKinley growled.

"That bad?"

McKinley rested his head on his front paws. "What do you smell?"

"Redburn. Some humans, but I don't know who. Something else. The wolf, perhaps? And . . . and gunpowder. Do I have it right?"

McKinley closed his eyes. "It was really awful."

"McKinley, every dog in town knows about the wolf. A few said they actually met her."

McKinley rolled his eyes at Aspen. "What are they saying?"

"It's a bit of a jumble. They seem to know Duchess was caught. And that Lupin was involved. That the wolf is trying to recruit dogs to her pack and . . ." She hesitated.

"Go on."

"They're excited. And worried. Asking about you, too. Wondering what you're doing. Some of the dogs believe you bungled everything, and . . ."

"And what?"

"Redburn beat you out."

McKinley growled again. "I suppose he's the one behind that story. This is what happened." He gave her the truth as he knew it.

When he was done, Aspen sighed. "Want some water? My outside bowl is full."

McKinley heaved himself up and followed his friend through the bushes to the back of her house. Though the water was a bit stale to his taste, he lapped it up. It soothed his mouth.

Aspen whimpered, "Now what are you going to do?"

"I need to see if I can get to Duchess. Hard to know what to do if I'm not even sure what happened."

"McKinley, have you considered doing nothing?"

Without even a look at her, McKinley began to trot off.

Aspen barked. "McKinley!"

He looked back.

"Be careful," she whined. "The dogs are upset. I bet the humans are, too. That wolf is making everyone nervous."

McKinley gave a sharp, single bark but continued on.

He was halfway to Elk Scat Way when he noticed two dogs standing by the wayside. One of them was a large poodle named Boots. The other was a Schnauzer-bulldog mix famous for his large, furry jowls. His owners, much to the dog's embarrassment, called him Jaws.

McKinley paused. The dogs were not reacting normally, offering respect to him as head dog. Boots cocked her ears and lifted her tail mockingly. Jaws even began to yip.

McKinley knew that if it came to a fight he would have no trouble with either of them, one at a time, or both together. All the same, he made a quick decision to trot on by.

"Hey, McKinley," Jaws barked, "you still head dog?"

McKinley refused to look back. But he knew that if they even asked such a question, it meant things were going to be different for a while— or forever.

When Pycraft's fence came into view, McKinley halted. He lifted his nose. Duchess's scent was strong, but she was nowhere in sight. For all McKinley knew she was trapped in the man's house. He followed the fence line sniffing the dirt. At the front corner he looked up and saw Duchess's leash dangling from its cable and running right into the doghouse.

McKinley trotted forward a few more paces, then paused. The doghouse, he realized, stood against the rear fence. If he could get behind that, he might be able to communicate directly with Duchess.

He ran back the way he had come, turned sharply at the next corner, and moved up Raccoon Way until he was behind the fence. There were some low, thick pine bushes crowding it. Slinking down on his belly, pulling himself ahead with his forepaws, and kicking with his rear legs, he was able to slither forward along the base of the fence.

It was not, he began thinking, a smart place to be. He could go forward, but a fast turnaround— in case he had to retreat—would be difficult. Still, he had to try reaching Duchess.

Once behind the doghouse he gave two short, low barks. "Duchess! It's me, McKinley. Can you hear me?" When there was no response he tried again, louder.

From inside the doghouse came a muffled "McKinley, that you?"

"It's me, all right. You okay?"

Duchess crept out into the open. Pulling at her restraining leash—doubled now—she slipped behind the doghouse. She lay down opposite McKinley, pushing her dry nose through the wires.

McKinley gave her nose a lick. "You hurt?"

Duchess whimpered. "Just miserable."

"Keep your voice down," McKinley growled. "And be calm. I'll find a way to get you out."

"McKinley," Duchess moaned, "they shot Lupin."

"How bad is she?"

"I'm not sure."

"Did she start back north?"

"I don't know."

"Is . . . is she going to live?"

"I don't know that, either."

"Duchess, I tried to help."

"I know you did," the greyhound whimpered. "See, I was supposed to lure Pycraft away so Lupin could run off and hide. It was her idea. But . . . but when I saw the long gun in that man's hand I got scared and messed things up. McKinley, what's going to happen to me? Or to Lupin? And you, too, McKinley. All the way home, Redburn was bragging that he was going to be head dog."

McKinley growled.

"Says he has the right to challenge you now. Does he?"

McKinley lifted his head. "Don't worry about me. I'm just trying to find a way to get you free."

"McKinley . . ."

"What?"

"Promise me something."

"Sure."

"Find Lupin. I never thought it would be possible, but she needs help."

"Will she accept it from me?"

"I . . . don't know. But promise you'll try to find her."

"The weather's changing. Could be snow."

"Please try."

"Okay. Sure. Don't worry about it."

Duchess sighed. "Thank you. It's just that I was so . . ." She started up, scrambled to her feet. "McKinley, Pycraft just came out of his house!"

# 14

McKinley could not see Pycraft, but he could smell him. He barely suppressed a growl.

"You dumb dog," the fat man shouted at Duchess. "Come on out from behind there."

McKinley heard the greyhound whimper.

"What do you think you're doing?" Pycraft demanded. "Not trying to escape again, were you? You're not going back to that wolf. He's a goner. Trying to steal you away. Not a chance. Now, come on, I'll feed you inside. That-a-girl. Here we go."

McKinley heard the man's steps recede, and a

door slam. He sniffed, then edged forward and peeked into the yard. No one was in sight.

Anxiously, McKinley dragged himself forward to the far side of the fence. Once there he shook his body free of leaves and dirt, then scampered away to safety.

After he'd turned down a couple of ways he stopped and tried to make sense of what he had heard Pycraft say. He was certain of the *wolf* word. There was anger in the man's voice, too. When humans were angry they did things. McKinley knew them well enough to know that when they did not like a dog, they sent him away or killed him. If Lupin hasn't gone, he thought, they will try to get rid of her, too. Or kill her.

McKinley wondered if Pycraft himself would do it. No, not alone. Not the type. With other humans, he thought. That would be good. The more people there were, the easier they would be to sniff out and avoid.

But still, he had to learn their plans. How, though?

Pycraft was the important one, but dealing with him was tricky. The man knew McKinley and would make instant trouble. It would be smarter to get another dog to go find the humans. Dogs could pretty much go where they wanted around Steamboat Springs. He'd find someone.

As for Lupin herself, he had promised Duchess he would try to help her. Perhaps she had already headed back to the wilderness up north? If it started snowing, all the better. Her tracks would be covered. But what if she was seriously wounded, and could not go? Snow wouldn't hide the scent of blood. Maybe she needed help just to stay alive.

Finally, there was Duchess. There had to be a way to free her for good.

As McKinley trotted on toward home, he let out a bark of frustration. With so much to do he found himself thinking again about what life would be like without people. The idea was becoming more and more tempting.

As he turned the corner onto Toward the Park Way, he halted. Waiting in the middle of the way, in front of Jack's house, was Redburn.

The big setter was standing tall, ears forward, nose wrinkled, bristling tail up. His lips were curled back, exposing his teeth. Here was the challenge McKinley had been warned to expect.

He stood quietly, body slightly sloped forward, front feet braced as he took in the situation. Feeling a surge of anger, McKinley lifted his head and let out a long howl, proclaiming to all who could hear him that this territory was his. Even as he howled, he once more remembered Lupin's cry and wished his was as strong.

Redburn did not flinch. He lifted his head and returned a howl as loud as McKinley's. He was not only challenging McKinley, he was calling on all the dogs in the pack to witness it.

With a low growl, McKinley began to move slowly toward Redburn.

"You're finished, McKinley," the setter barked without giving way. "No one wants you as head dog anymore. Step aside and submit, or we can fight it out right now."

McKinley took a deep breath. Might as well fight now, he thought. "I know what I want," he growled, and moved forward again.

"I'm ready," Redburn returned with a snarl.

Just then McKinley saw Aspen burst through the bushes. As soon as she took in what was happening, her tail drooped. She began to bark rapidly.

"Shut up!" Redburn snapped at her. "This is between McKinley and me. We don't need anyone else."

Aspen looked toward McKinley. He gave a curt nod. She closed her mouth.

The next moment Boots and Jaws came galloping down the way, barking with excitement. "A fight! A fight!" As soon as they saw McKinley and Redburn, they skidded to a stop.

"Redburn!" McKinley growled. "I'll give you a chance to go now. Either you do or I'll send you away with your tail between your legs."

"I don't think so," Redburn returned. "And

when I become head dog you'll go to the bottom of the pack, where you can lick my paws."

From the other side of the way Tubbs suddenly appeared. "Hey," he barked, looking from McKinley to Redburn. "What are you guys doing?"

"Keep out of the way, runt-foot," Redburn growled.

"Oh . . . yeah, sure," Tubbs whimpered. Hastily, he backed up, tail drooping, eyes lowered.

McKinley leaned forward on the tips of his claws. The hair along his back and his erect tail bristled. Teeth exposed, he looked at Redburn coldly, trying to decide exactly where to attack. He was close enough to feel the setter's breath.

A loud noise erupted behind him—the sound of a truck—followed by the long beep of an auto horn.

"McKinley!" came a shout. It was the female, Sarah. "McKinley, what do you think you're doing?" she cried.

Reluctantly, Redburn broke off the challenge. Growling, "Lucky you," he backed away from McKinley.

But McKinley lunged forward, only to feel himself held back by Sarah's strong hands on his collar.

"Stop it, McKinley!" she cried. "No fighting! Scoot, Redburn," she yelled at the setter. "Get home to your own street! Now get!"

Redburn turned his back on McKinley and walked off a few feet, then paused and looked over his shoulder. "McKinley, you refused a fair fight. I'm calling a meeting of the pack. Like it or not, I'm going to be the new head dog."

Showing his teeth, McKinley tried to leap forward again. Sarah restrained him.

Redburn trotted off, leg feathers flowing. The sight enraged McKinley. He struggled to get free.

"Stop this!" Sarah demanded. "I won't have you fighting. If you do, I'll lock you inside the house."

McKinley sat. He opened his mouth slightly and stuck out his tongue. From the corner of his eye he saw Boots and Jaws scamper away. They would, he knew, spread the news.

"There. That's better," the woman said, letting go of McKinley's collar. "We have quite enough dog business in town without fighting. There's a meeting over at the town hall right now about that wolf Jack saw. Now, are you going to be calm?" she asked McKinley.

The *wolf.* He put up a paw and touched her knee, whimpering softly to tell her he was fine.

"Good boy," Sarah said. She got back in her truck and drove it close to the house. Then she went inside, carrying food. McKinley could smell fresh meat.

As he watched her, Aspen hurried up. "Are you all right?"

"Fine."

Tubbs came as well. "Oh, wow, McKinley. That was serious."

McKinley looked down at him. "Tubbs, I've got an important job for you."

"You do?"

"If I understood my female right, I think the humans are having a gathering to talk about Lupin."

"Who's Lupin?"

"That wolf you were asking about. Find that

gathering. No one will mind you being there. Figure out what they are planning about the wolf."

"Me?" Tubbs yelped, his tail wagging furiously. "You want *me* to do that?"

"Yes."

"Oh, wow. Thanks. Well, sure, I think I can. Absolutely. I will. Right now?"

"Now."

Tubbs went scrambling down the way, barking with pleasure.

McKinley turned to Aspen. "I need your help, too."

"What kind?"

"I have to find Lupin. But I'd feel better if you came with me, just in case."

"In case of what?"

"Aspen, she's a lot more powerful than I am. She might turn on me. If something happened to me I'd want the pack to know about it. Will you come?"

Aspen looked into McKinley's eyes. "Of course."

Side by side they began to lope toward Strawberry Park.

# 15

McKinley checked the little house on Fox Haven Way. There were no new messages. With Aspen still by his side, he plunged across the field and up into the hills.

Aspen sniffed. "Where was Duchess hiding?"

McKinley pointed his nose toward the boulders. "There's a place inside all these rocks. Lupin was in there, too. When Duchess came out—here— Pycraft grabbed her. Redburn and Sullivan—with the long gun—were over there. And here"— McKinley smelled the area below the boulders— "Aspen," he barked. "Smell here."

Aspen put her nose down, then looked up. "Blood."

McKinley growled. "I bet it's Lupin's. It all happened pretty fast, but she ran around here." He trotted behind the boulders, Aspen following close. "Being out front, I didn't see what happened. But when I heard two explosions, I took off."

Aspen barked. "I'm glad you did."

"There's blood here, too."

Aspen drew closer. "Still Lupin's?"

"Pretty sure. The trail leads over here." McKinley worked his way through the bushes, nose low, taking deep breaths as he went.

Aspen kept up with McKinley's zigzag patterns, now and again darting off on her own.

Lupin's scent led them higher into the hills.

"She sure wasn't traveling a straight line," Aspen barked. "Think she was heading north?"

McKinley looked around. "Maybe. Looks like she was trying to cover her tracks."

Aspen put her nose to the earth. "I don't smell anyone following."

"Right. Redburn was really scared when he got a whiff of her. Unless Sullivan made him, he never would have gone on his own. But I think the humans were scared, too."

Aspen gazed at him. "McKinley, you're scared of her, too, aren't you?"

"Yes. But in a different way."

"What way?"

"I'm not sure."

"What *are* you going to do about Redburn?"

"His challenge? Unless he backs down, I have to accept it."

"Could . . . could he beat you?"

McKinley cocked his head at her. With a snort he bent down over his forelegs, lifted his rump, wagged his tail, then leaped up and landed on Aspen's back, taking her by enough surprise to knock her over. Barking, she pulled away, got up, frisked sideways, then back again so that she came down on him, sending him sprawling. Yelping together, they rolled down the hill, nipping and mouthing each other excitedly. Then, tongues lolling, panting, they stood free and faced each other, tails wagging.

Aspen barked, "I thought this was supposed to be serious."

McKinley leaned forward and licked her nose. "Always time for fun."

Aspen opened her mouth and gently bit his muzzle. Then she flopped down and rolled onto her back while whimpering softly. McKinley pushed his nose into the folds of skin around her neck and gave her an affectionate nip.

Aspen spun over, and for a minute they gazed into each other's eyes, tails slowly wagging.

It was McKinley who broke away to look back up the hill. "We better get going."

Aspen barked her agreement.

McKinley climbed to the spot where they last had a whiff of the wolf's scent. "This way!" He began to follow the trail again toward Buffalo Pass. Aspen kept a step behind.

After a while she paused. "I think Lupin's lost a lot of blood."

McKinley growled. "She's sure slowed down. She can't be too far from here."

Aspen held back. "McKinley, do you really think she'd attack you?"

"Don't know. When I first met her she was really angry. But now she's hurt, probably weak. If she were a dog . . . but she's a wolf."

They pressed on, coming to an area so thick with pines, most sunlight was blocked out. The air was chilly.

McKinley stopped. "Hold it!"

Aspen drew even with her friend. "What is it?"

"See that huge pine tree that's fallen over straight ahead? The one with the roots exposed?"

"What about it?"

"Can't you sniff it? Lupin's trail leads right there. I smell water, too. Must be a little creek nearby. If I were hurt and looking to hide, I'd want to be near water, wouldn't you? She must be close. Come on."

"McKinley, careful . . ."

Nose to the ground, though occasionally looking up and around, McKinley moved forward.

Near the fallen pine he halted. When the tree fell, its roots had ripped out of the earth.

McKinley moved forward cautiously. "There's some sort of hole under those roots. And a strong smell of blood. I think Lupin is hiding there."

Aspen lifted her nose. "Doesn't smell like death."

They drew within a dog's length of the roots, then sat.

After a moment McKinley barked by way of greeting. "It's me, Lupin. McKinley!"

When there was no response he barked again. "Lupin, we've come to help. Can you hear me?"

From the hole beneath the torn-up roots a low growl sounded.

Aspen stood up, whimpered, and took a step back. McKinley barked again. "We really want to help!"

As they watched the hole, two eyes appeared, staring out from the darkest shadow. Lupin. Her mouth was open. Her teeth glistened. "What do you want, dogs?" she snarled.

McKinley stood.

Both dogs lowered their heads with respect and let their tails droop.

"Lupin, I've come to help," McKinley tried again. "Are you badly hurt?"

"Your humans shot me."

Aspen barked, "You've lost a lot of blood, haven't you?"

Lupin glared at her. "Who are you?"

"My name is Aspen. I'm McKinley's friend."

"McKinley's friend . . . I tried to help his friend, Duchess. But a slave dog led his master to where we were."

McKinley growled. "That was Redburn. I tried to keep him from doing it."

"You failed, dog."

"I know that. Lupin, how badly hurt are you?"

"I've bled some. My shoulder is in pain, and it's hard for me to move. I'm hungry, too. There's a creek just over there. It's as far as I could go. This is what comes of dealing with your humans. McKinley, why do they hate wolves so? Is it because we refuse to be their slaves?"

"Maybe it's because you look like a dog but you're wild. That confuses people. Can we bring you some food?"

"I'm a meat eater," Lupin growled. "Real meat. Fresh meat. I'd rather die than eat the rubbish you dogs eat."

Aspen and McKinley exchanged looks.

McKinley lifted his eyes to the wolf. "If we get fresh meat for you, will you eat?"

"If it's real, yes." Lupin sounded weaker.

"I'll get you some." McKinley trotted off a ways.

Aspen followed him. "What are you going to do?"

"Get what she wants."

Aspen wagged her tail. "Maybe I better stay here."

"You sure?"

"McKinley, I think she's worse than she lets on. She might need me to bring water."

McKinley looked at his friend with admiration. "I'll get back as quick as I can."

# 16

McKinley raced down the hill to Fox Haven Way, then moved along Porcupine Way above the pups' gathering place. He saw no sign of Jack—which was good, because the pup was the last one McKinley wanted around. He looked up. Clouds were coming in. The sun's position suggested midafternoon. A smell of snow was in the air. He needed to hurry. The boy would be coming home soon.

Outside his house McKinley looked and sniffed for any clue that the man or woman were home. Neither the car nor truck was parked out front.

Relieved, he worked the front door open and slipped inside.

Once in the hallway he took a deep breath. No humans. To be absolutely sure, he barked a few times, something he was not supposed to do inside. He checked the sleeping rooms. No one. But in Jack's room, piled up in a corner, was a pile of the things Jack took when he went into the woods and slept: his large foot coverings, a bottle, his new backpack.

Seeing that the pup was serious about finding Lupin and going with her, McKinley sighed with frustration. Though he knew it was his job to stop him, he had to deal with the wolf first.

He hurried to the food place, lifted his head, and sniffed. The room smelled of the food Sarah had recently brought into the house. Particularly strong was the smell of fresh meat—just as he had hoped.

Usually, humans' meat was kept in the box that was cold. A few times, using paws and jaws, McKinley had opened its door just out of curiosity.

Not that he had ever removed anything from inside. That would be *bad*. But today he was dealing with an emergency.

After a small struggle he worked the door open. But McKinley knew from the chilly smells that the meat he was looking for wasn't there.

This was puzzling. Using his front paws for support, McKinley stood on his hind legs and peered along the flat places where the people mixed up their food. What he saw was a deep, shining bowl. Though covered, a strong smell of meat was coming from it. The meat was there. But could he get to it?

Even as McKinley had the thought, he felt guilty. What he was attempting to do, was, by every house rule, *very bad*. Just to think of the humans' anger caused him to hang his head and lower his tail.

But he had to save Lupin.

McKinley made two attempts to jump up to the bowl. But there was no room to make a running start.

Maybe he could get to the bowl by pushing it forward to the edge of the flat place. He had to try, so he jumped up to where Jack sat to eat and, using his forepaws, pulled himself along the back of it. With his rear legs he kicked himself up onto the narrow place where the humans kept the talking thing. It went crashing to the floor.

Heart thumping, McKinley squeezed over the top of the box that was cold until he reached the far side. The bowl was just below him now. He was about to jump down when he heard a voice:

"If you would like to make a call, please hang up and dial again."

McKinley froze. Neither sight, sound, nor smell suggested anyone had come into the room.

Even so, the voice came again:

"If you would like to make a call, please hang up and dial again."

McKinley peered down to the floor. When the voice spoke another time he realized it was coming from the talking thing. But now the thing began to chirp. He decided to ignore it.

Stealthfully, McKinley dropped down from the top of the cold box onto the food-mixing place, where the shiny bowl sat.

It was covered by a plate with a loop on the top. McKinley grasped the loop in his mouth and lifted. It came up with ease. Twisting about, he dropped it—*crash*—onto the counter.

McKinley peered into the bowl. A hunk of meat was soaking in shallow, sour-smelling water. But then, as McKinley knew, people did strange things with their food.

He leaned into the bowl, grasped the meat firmly with his teeth, and lifted it out. He was just about to leap down from the mixing place when he thought about keeping neat. Humans liked that. What he was doing was bad enough. So he dropped the meat to the floor—*splat*—then picked the plate up with his teeth and returned it to the top of the bowl.

Only then did he leap down to the floor.

Hurriedly, McKinley licked the floor clean. Though the water tasted bitter, he didn't care. He snatched up the meat with his teeth and headed for the front door. There was nothing he could do about the talking thing.

He was just approaching the door when it swung open.

There was Jack. "McKinley!" he cried. "What are you doing with that meat?"

Springing forward, McKinley dashed past the boy, out the door, and down the way, the meat clenched tightly in his teeth.

"McKinley! Come back here, you bad dog. Come back!"

# 17

Without a pause, McKinley ran to Strawberry Park, up into the hills, and to the tumbled pine. There he found Aspen stretched out before the exposed tree roots, head on her forepaws. Lupin was nowhere in sight.

McKinley growled to announce his arrival. Aspen looked up and around as he—wagging his tail for her—stepped into the clearing.

"Where'd you get that?" Aspen barked.

McKinley dropped the meat onto the ground. "Don't ask. Where's Lupin?"

Aspen nodded toward the exposed roots. "She's

very weak. She was thirsty, too, but when I offered to get her some water, she refused. Insisted upon crawling out and dragging herself to the creek. The effort exhausted her. I don't think she could do it again."

McKinley went to the hole and looked down. Lupin lay four feet below, curled up in a ball, tail over her face. The smell of blood and sickness was strong.

McKinley barked a few times. "Lupin! It's me, McKinley. I've brought you some food."

Ears flicking, the wolf lifted her head a few inches only to growl softly and lower her head again.

"No, really," McKinley whined. "It's what you asked for. Food."

Lupin managed to snarl, "No dog food," without moving.

McKinley stared at her for a moment, then turned to where the meat lay, picked it up, and carried it to the edge of the hole.

"Lupin, it's real meat. I took it from my humans.

Smell it for yourself." He held the meat with his teeth over the hole.

The wolf raised her head and sniffed. Her eyes were only partially open, and dull. Her nose looked dry.

Lupin growled again. "It smells strange."

"My humans were soaking it in something. But it's still meat. And it's fresh."

With a groan, Lupin labored to her feet. But when she made an attempt to lift herself out of the hole, she fell back.

Aspen put her mouth next to McKinley's ear. "I don't think she can do it."

McKinley peered down at Lupin. "Then we'll have to get her out. If we don't, she'll die in there. Lupin, I'm coming down!"

He leaped into the hole. The stench of the wolf's wound was almost unbearable. At one shoulder the fur had been torn away. The exposed skin was filthy, clotted with dried blood, oozing a horrible-smelling wetness. But McKinley saw that Lupin could not get at it to keep the wound clean. He shook his head in dismay. "You must get out of here, Lupin. Try pulling yourself up. I'll push you from below."

Lupin turned to look at him. "Dog—"

"Lupin," McKinley snapped, "you've got to move."

Snarling, Lupin slowly came to her feet.

There was little room for both of them, but McKinley managed to wedge his head under the wolf's rear and began to push up. The wolf was enormously heavy. She seemed to be making no effort to help herself.

Aspen peered down from above. "Can you help her?"

McKinley looked up. "She's deadweight."

To Lupin, he barked, "Don't give up! If you stay down here, you'll die. Is that what you want? What's the point of being free if you're dead?"

Lupin lowered her head and drew back her lips to reveal her teeth in a show of anger. But then her mouth slackened. Her eyes closed. Turning, she lifted her head toward the opening of the hole.

Aspen was still looking down.

McKinley yelped, "I'll push. You pull!"

"I understand."

"Lupin," he bayed, "come on!" He ducked his head under her and began to shove upward again.

Lupin struggled to stand on her hind feet. Then she used her still good leg to raise and steady herself.

Panting from exertion, McKinley shoved with all his strength. "That's it. That's it!"

He saw the wolf hook her good paw over the top of the hole and pull. After a nervous moment, Aspen reached down, gripped the ruff of Lupin's neck in her teeth, and began to haul up—just enough for McKinley to quickly shift his position. Now he was using his whole broad back to help the wolf claw upward—drawing dirt into the hole—while Aspen pulled. The higher Lupin went, the more McKinley arched his back.

Aspen gave one final yank, and the panting wolf flopped over the edge of the hole. But her hindquarters still dangled down.

Standing up, McKinley used his head to push

harder as Aspen worked to drag the wolf away from the hole.

With a final grunt Lupin rolled completely out.

Leaping, scratching, and scrambling, McKinley managed to get himself out of the hole. Once up, he shook himself free of dirt.

He and Aspen examined Lupin. She lay stretched on the ground in a heap, breathing hard. Her eyes were closed.

McKinley placed the meat before her nose. The wolf—eyes still closed—lifted her nose an inch and sniffed. Opening her mouth, she made a feeble snap at the meat but missed.

McKinley looked around at Aspen.

"I think I know what to do," she whimpered. Placing one paw on the meat, she bit off a chunk and began to chew it.

"Aspen, it's for her!" McKinley snapped.

Aspen continued to chew. When she had softened the meat into a pulp, she spat it out onto the ground in front of Lupin's nose.

The wolf sniffed at the chewed meat. First she

licked it, then she extended her open mouth. But she was too weak to draw the food in. While McKinley watched, Aspen nosed the food directly into the wolf's mouth.

After a moment Lupin began to chew and then swallow quickly.

McKinley looked over at Aspen. "How'd you know to do that?"

She wagged her tail. "It's what wolves do for their pups. And we're all partly wolves—right?"

McKinley made no response.

But as Lupin fed, he sniffed her wound. It was so dirty, he couldn't tell how serious it was. He began to lick at it, then pull away the torn flesh gently, spitting out the foul bits and using his rough tongue to clean the remaining filth.

Lupin lay still, only now and again whimpering softly.

**18**

Twice, McKinley went for water. The creek was a small one, more a soggy mess of leaves and twigs with a few pools than a free-flowing brook. But at one of the pools McKinley lapped up water, filled his mouth, and carried it back to Lupin. With some coaxing, Aspen got the wolf to lift her head so McKinley could dump the water directly into her mouth.

When the wolf had consumed all the meat and taken some more drink, she rested. Now and again she looked up, staring first at Aspen, then at McKinley. Though her eyes had brightened, she did not speak. Nor wag her tail. Finally, she curled up into a ball and fell into a deep sleep.

The sky was growing dark.

McKinley turned to Aspen. "What do you think?"

"She's a little better. But not by much."

McKinley knew their humans would be wondering where they were.

Aspen sighed. "Do you think we can leave her?"

McKinley growled. "I'm sure people are going to come hunt for her. If she stays here she'll be awfully easy to find. And it's getting colder. I think we're in for some snow."

"What do you want to do, then?"

McKinley stood up, facing first one direction then another. Suddenly he wagged his tail.

"Have an idea?"

"Do you think we could get her to move?"

"Not far."

"I'll be right back!" McKinley began to run down the hill.

He burst out of the woods and galloped across the field, slowing only when he approached the little house. Though the place looked deserted, as it usually did, McKinley wanted to be certain. Tilting his ears forward, he listened and sniffed deeply. Nothing. To make doubly sure, he barked, but no response came.

Turning, he scampered up the way that ran before the house and after a short run leaped off it. It was here that the creek, which curved close, was fed by a trickle running down off the hills. Maybe, McKinley thought, it's the same water as Lupin's.

McKinley jumped into the creek. The cold water reached his knees. Confident that he was leaving no scent, except on the way he had bounded over, he splashed forward.

When the creek turned behind the little house, McKinley jumped, landing on a flat surface of many wooden boards. Excitedly, he ran up and down in search of a means to get inside the house. There was a door, but it was closed. He couldn't budge it. But near the door he saw a small window covered by some thin, torn cloth. It looked to be too high for him. McKinley whined with frustration.

Pacing around, he discovered a small, four-legged platform. He nudged it under the window, jumped up, and stood on his hind legs. The window was now in reach. Gripping the cloth with his teeth, McKinley pulled at it and it came away easily. The window, he saw, was a sliding one that opened from side to side.

Barking with excitement, McKinley used his nose like a wedge and moved the window open. That done, he jumped off the platform and trotted as far from the opening as possible. Then he ran . . . and leaped. His aim was perfect. Front legs curled under his body, head extended, nose pointing, he flew right into the little house.

There was something blocking him on the other side of the window. It went over with a crash, but McKinley managed to land safely. He scrambled to his feet, gave himself a shake, and looked around.

He had landed in a room containing two small, soft sitting places that faced each other. On one wall was a large window, covered over with some hanging stuff. Against another wall stood the long, narrow snow sliders that humans use, big shoes close by. There was a closed front door. But the human smells were stale, old. People had not been here for a long while.

McKinley trotted around a corner. There he saw the kind of layered box that people crammed things into, an open space full of hanging body coverings, and a large, soft sleeping place.

Satisfied with what he'd found, McKinley ran back into the first room, then down a hallway, passing a water room before reaching a small food surface. The cold box was open but not cold. There was no food inside.

Still, he was sure the house was the perfect place to hide Lupin—if he could get her inside. That was the problem. In her weakness, she could not make the jump he'd made to get in.

McKinley studied the front door. Different from doors he knew, he could see no way of opening it. He looked at the rear door, the one that led to the large wooden surface. What he saw was a door handle just like the one in Jack's house.

He approached it, stood on his rear legs while holding himself erect with his front paws, gripped the knob in his jaws, and twisted. When the doorknob turned, he pulled back, and the door opened.

Barking with delight, McKinley slipped out. Barely pausing, he plunged back into the creek, retraced his steps, and headed up into the hills.

He crashed into the clearing, barking. "How's Lupin doing?"

Aspen wagged her tail. "Better, I think. She's got some wetness on her nose. And she seems to be sleeping soundly." She sniffed. "Where have you been? I can't place it."

"I found a hideout for her. You know that little house on Fox Haven Way? Right below us?"

"Yes."

"In there."

Aspen growled. "Are you serious?"

"Aspen, think about it. It's empty. No humans are around. They won't use the place until snow comes. And they would never think of looking for a wolf in one of their own houses."

"How would she get in?"

"I can't open the front door. But I left a back one open."

Aspen gazed at McKinley, then turned to the sleeping wolf and sighed. "I suppose we could try."

His tail lowered out of respect, McKinley approached Lupin. He barked once, then twice.

Lupin opened her eyes and looked up at him, but made no sound.

McKinley drew closer. "Lupin, you can't stay here. There's a good chance the humans will come looking for you. But you're too weak to run, so you need to hide. I found a great place."

The wolf growled. "Where?"

Suddenly nervous, McKinley yawned. "It's downhill and just out of these woods. In a small . . . human house."

Lupin wrinkled her nose and growled again, making a deeper sound than before. "Dog, you are such a fool. Do you know how I got my limp?"

"No."

"Humans." She lifted her crooked leg. "I've been shot twice, now."

"Lupin, listen to me. You're hurt. You can't move fast. Not yet. If people come, they'll find you. You won't be able to defend yourself."

The wolf was silent.

McKinley allowed himself a small growl. "Lupin, if you stay here, you'll die."

After a moment the wolf turned toward McKinley. "If I can't stay here, I'll go back to my own wilderness." She labored to her feet. Her body swayed. And when she took a tentative step, her legs trembled.

McKinley whimpered. "You see, you're not strong enough now to make it."

Lupin looked around at Aspen. "What do you think?"

Aspen wagged her tail. "I think McKinley is right."

Lupin shook her massive head and sighed. "Very well. I'll go."

# 19

Lupin limped slowly in McKinley's tracks.

Aspen barked, "Isn't the house the other way, McKinley?"

He lifted his head. "I'm going to follow the water downhill. We don't want to leave a trail."

He led them to the trickling stream where he had fetched water for Lupin. As soon as they reached it, the wolf lapped some up.

McKinley continued to lead, though it was Lupin who set the pace. Now and again McKinley turned back to look at the wolf in the fading light. Her head low, tail drooping, she was clearly in pain. Though she made no complaint, she often paused to moisten her mouth.

When the three reached the edge of the trees, they halted. A wind was rising.

Lupin lifted her nose and sniffed. "Humans."

Aspen drew closer to the wolf. "Around here you can always smell people. But I don't think anyone is close."

"I despise humans," Lupin growled.

McKinley looked about. "They're not all bad."

"Then why must I hide?" Lupin snapped.

"To tell the truth, Lupin, it's not the humans I'm worried about. It's the dogs."

The wolf turned her head. "What do you mean?"

Aspen answered her. "Remember, it was a dog who led that human with the long gun to you."

Lupin was silent for a moment. Then she snarled, "It's because you dogs allow yourselves to become slaves to humans that such things happen."

McKinley decided not to respond. "Wait here. I need to be sure no one's around."

He trotted out from beneath the trees into the

field. The moon, obscured by thickening clouds, cast a dull glow on the high, dry grass. No stars were visible. McKinley sniffed. Snow was certainly coming.

Returning to where Aspen and Lupin waited, he barked, "We can go on."

They splashed quietly along until they reached the cabin.

"Here we are," McKinley barked.

Lupin squinted at the building and wrinkled her nose with loathing. "Do you expect me to go in there?" she growled angrily.

"Lupin, you can't stay outside," McKinley reminded her. "But if people come, they'll never think to look here. It's the safest place."

"What about dogs?"

"We've been walking in water. No scent."

Lupin continued to gaze at the house. "I've never been in a . . . house before."

Aspen cocked her head. "It won't be so bad."

"How do you expect me to get into it?"

McKinley gazed at the wolf. "There's a back door. I left it open."

Lupin turned toward him. "What's a door?"

"It's a flat board that swings and lets you into houses but keeps the weather out."

Lupin shook her head, nothing more.

With much shoving and pulling, Aspen and McKinley eased Lupin onto the wooden surface behind the house.

McKinley nudged the back door open wider. He and Aspen went inside. Lupin hung back in the dark. "It stinks of people," she growled.

Aspen stuck her head out of the door and licked the wolf's nose. "Lupin, you'll be safe. And warm."

The wolf, her head low, tail bristling, sniffing in an agitated manner, moved cautiously forward. Once inside, she turned to look back at the door.

McKinley noticed. "When we leave, you can close the door, mostly. Just make sure you keep it open a crack. That way—if you have to—you can always get out."

Lupin growled, "Where am I to sleep?"

"Most comfortable place in the world. Follow me."

McKinley led the way into the far room.

"What's that?"

"A soft sleeping place," Aspen barked. She jumped on it and began to pummel the thick covering with her paws. "Try it. It's really nice."

"I don't need niceness," Lupin grunted.

McKinley was beginning to feel weary. "Lupin, you can sleep anywhere you want."

"What about food?" the wolf wanted to know. "Water?"

McKinley left the others and checked the water room. The low bowl was full of water. He came back. "Plenty of water up front. And we'll bring you food in the morning."

Avoiding the soft sleeping place, a tense Lupin limped back into the room with the two doors. She sat awkwardly.

McKinley and Aspen started for the back door.

"McKinley! Aspen!" Lupin barked sharply.

The two dogs looked around.

The wolf had closed her eyes. "Have either of you ever lived in the forest?"

"No, neither of us."

Lupin sighed. "Out there," she growled softly, "in the wilderness, there are no walls. Overhead is the sun, or clouds, or the moon. At night there are as many stars in the sky as there are stones on earth. The moon glides between the trees before leaping up. Water runs free. Food is where you find it. What you eat you have earned because you have worked to catch it. You live in a river of many smells, smells that are constantly changing, that bring you news of the entire world. You are part of that world. Always."

The wolf lay down, head resting on her fore-paws. "But here . . . ," she whimpered, "all is enclosed. Like . . . like an old nut in a hard shell."

McKinley and Aspen remained still.

Lupin growled. "Why are you leaving me?"

It was Aspen who answered. "You couldn't stay where you were. But you can't come into town. And we need to be in our homes."

"Why?" Lupin persisted.

McKinley whimpered. "The humans depend on us, too."

Lupin shook her head, then closed her eyes.

After a moment Aspen and McKinley went toward the back door. "Remember," McKinley warned, "don't shut the door completely. Otherwise you won't be able to get out."

Lupin looked toward the front door. "That one is closed."

Aspen shook her head. "You only need one way out."

"Don't worry," McKinley added. "You'll be perfectly safe."

"McKinley! Aspen!"

They paused.

"If one of those people does come here," Lupin growled, "I won't go easy."

"No one will come."

Aspen followed McKinley out onto the wooden surface. Once beyond the door, they waited.

Behind them, the door shut with a click.

Aspen looked around. "What's that click mean?"

McKinley sighed. "She shut the door too hard. It's locked."

"Don't you think you should open it?"

McKinley thought a moment. "I can always use the window. Be better if she stays. She can't survive on her own. Not yet."

Aspen gazed at McKinley, who only turned from her, toward the stream. In silence, they waded back into it, then took the dirt way toward town.

They had not traveled far before Aspen stopped. "Now that Lupin's safe, what do you intend to do?"

"Feed her until she's strong enough to return home on her own. Can you get some food? I'm going to be in big trouble about that when I get home."

"I can try."

As they trotted down their way, Tubbs, tail wagging, waddled toward them. "Where have you two been?" he barked.

Weary, McKinley sat. "Taking care of business."

Tubbs drew closer but suddenly halted. His tail drooped. His nose wrinkled. "What's that smell?"

"The wolf."

"Have . . . have you been with her?"

McKinley barked once.

"I sure hope she's gone."

"Why?"

"Don't you remember? You asked me to go to the human's gathering? Well, I did."

"And . . . ?"

"At their big meeting place there were lots of people. Lots of excitement. A few dogs, too. Redburn was there."

"Tubbs, just tell us what happened," McKinley snapped.

"I am, McKinley. But, you know how it is: I had to put together the words I understood. I'm pretty sure, though, a bunch of people are going to hunt that wolf. I mean, I heard the word *wolf* lots of times. Same for *hunt*. A few of those humans even brought long guns to that meeting. So I think I got it right. And I'm pretty sure Redburn is supposed to lead them."

McKinley and Aspen glanced at one another.

"When are they going?"

"I heard *tomorrow*. And *morning*, too. Did . . . did I do good, McKinley? Did I?"

"You did great, Tubbs. Thanks."

McKinley turned to Aspen. "We better meet here tomorrow, early."

"Oh!" Tubbs barked. "I forgot something."

"What's that?"

"I think Pycraft is in charge of the hunt."

"What makes you so sure?"

"He was doing most of the word saying. He sounded really angry."

McKinley sighed. "I guess we'll just have to make sure nothing bad happens." He turned toward his house. "See you in the morning."

Both Aspen and Tubbs barked a good night.

McKinley opened the front door and trotted down the hallway toward the food place. Jack and his parents were sitting around their food platform.

McKinley, tail wagging, approached meekly.

"McKinley!" Jack cried. "Where you been, you *bad dog*. Stealing our dinner!"

All three humans looked at him severely.

"Now you know why it wasn't so great teaching him to open doors," Gil said to Jack.

"I didn't!"

"Well, somebody did."

McKinley felt obliged to hang his head and droop his tail.

"McKinley," the female announced, "consider yourself in prison. Tomorrow, it's indoors for you. All day. You're grounded."

*Grounded.* That, too, was a word McKinley knew and understood.

# 20

McKinley lay on the floor of Jack's room, ears alert. Though he kept his head on his forelegs, his eyes were fixed upward on the pup.

The boy was in his soft sleeping place, a cloth over his body, head propped up by one hand. A light glowed over his head, and staring papers rested on his lump of softness. But the boy wasn't staring at the papers. He was gazing back at McKinley.

"McKinley," he scolded in a whisper, "why did you *do* that?"

McKinley, wanting to cheer the boy up, wagged his tail a few times.

"Do you know how much I *love* pot roast?" the boy complained. "Do you have any idea how unusual that is around here? Like, once a month? Like, once a year?"

McKinley sighed. He did not know what the boy was saying, but he knew a scolding when he heard it.

"And another thing, McKinley," Jack went on. "People know about the wolf. Dad said it all has to do with that dog, Duchess. And that you were there when they found her and the wolf. Is that true? Why didn't you take me? Now there's this hunt on to get the wolf tomorrow morning. A lot of stupid people are going. Like that nasty Mr. Pycraft. You know what *that* means?"

McKinley studied Jack's face, trying to make sense of the words he understood: *Wolf. Dad. Found. Hunt. Pycraft.*

"If I don't get to the wolf first," the boy continued, "I'll never be able to go off with him. Those people will kill him. So guess what? I'm going tomorrow, really early. Before those hunters. See, if I can get to the wolf, I'll warn him off, then follow him back to his pack. What do you think?"

McKinley had caught the words *go, get, find, kill, follow, home*. Was the boy going to look for Lupin the next day? Was that it? But why would he say *kill?*

Suddenly, Jack jumped out of his sleeping place, went to his clothing storage box, and slid the door open. McKinley could see that the backpack was stuffed. And attached to the top was the bundle Gil crawled into when he slept outside.

"See," the boy said to McKinley. "I'm ready to go."

*Ready* and *go*. Head cocked, McKinley looked from the backpack to the pup.

"Oh, McKinley, I wish you could understand me!" Jack cried. He pointed to his chest. "*Me*. I'm going to the *wolf. Tomorrow.*"

This was what McKinley had understood before. The pup was going to Lupin. But now he seemed to be going *tomorrow*. Did that mean Jack knew where the wolf was hiding?

Horrified, McKinley whimpered and put a paw on the boy's arm to restrain him.

"I set my alarm for five o'clock," Jack explained, squeezing the large paw affectionately. "But you can't go. You'd probably scare that old wolf, anyway."

The pup returned to his soft place, got under the cloth, and clicked the light off. "Wish me luck, buddy," he whispered in the dark.

Wagging his tail, McKinley pushed his snout forward and gave Jack a lick on the face.

"No, McKinley, you can't come with me," the pup said. "You're a bad dog."

Backing away, McKinley headed out of the room. Why was he bad? And how would he be able to keep the boy from running off to Lupin?

He padded his way into the food place, where he lapped up some water from his bowl. A faint smell of meat clung to the floor. Feeling guilty, he gave the spots a couple of licks.

In the front room the male and female were watching the fluttering glow box, which as always gave off a faint smell of burning. Why humans stared at it so much was something McKinley never had understood.

He lay down at the woman's feet, and rolled his eyes up at her. Why was she paying so little attention to her boy? How could he tell her what Jack was planning?

Sarah glanced down at him. "I hope you understand what you did, McKinley," she said, sounding stern. "Though, I must admit, you are clever, putting the pot cover back on. I suppose you thought you could fool us. And you know what, McKinley? Keeping you in all day is going to be one big nuisance."

The man, eyes fixed on the glow box, said, "Honey, McKinley doesn't understand a word you're saying."

"Oh, probably more than we think," she replied.

McKinley sat up and barked.

"See?" the female said with a laugh.

McKinley had an idea. If he could lead either the male or female to Jack's clothing box, they might see the backpack and understand what their pup was about to do. Why couldn't they be smarter? He took hold of Sarah's clothing and gave it a tug.

"Scoot, McKinley," she said, shaking her sleeve free. "I don't want to play."

McKinley trotted to the food place door and barked.

"McKinley!" Gil cried. "Be quiet. I'm trying to watch the news."

Discouraged, McKinley came back into the room, lay down, closed his eyes, and sighed. There were times—and this was one of them—he wished the responsibility for the pup wasn't just his.

Gradually another idea came. McKinley knew it meant trouble—but it should keep the boy from going and allow *him* to help Lupin. If that made him a bad dog, so be it. It had to be done.

When McKinley woke, the glow box was dark. The room was cooler, quiet. He lifted his head and listened. No one was moving about. He could hear the gentle breathing of sleep in the house.

He stood and stretched. In the food place he took a few nibbles of the dried biscuit bits left in his bowl, and followed that up with a lap of water.

Down the hall he saw only a faint light by the door to Jack's water room.

Trotting over to his sleeping place, McKinley rested his chin on the cloth covering. Yes, the pup was asleep.

Silently, McKinley went to the clothing box. With a forepaw, he slid the door open. The backpack lay on the floor. McKinley gripped one of the straps in his teeth and began to chew. The strap tasted awful, and it was tough, but soon he had bitten it into two pieces. He started working on another strap.

The pup stirred and suddenly sat up. "McKinley?" he called. "That you?"

McKinley got up and went to the sleeping place.

"What are you doing?" Jack asked in a sleepy voice.

McKinley licked the pup's face.

"Good boy," Jack murmured, and gave him a hug. Then he flopped down and fell asleep again.

McKinley went back to the backpack and continued his work.

As soon as the last strap was chewed, McKinley checked on the pup. Still sleeping.

Satisfied, McKinley quit the room and crept to the front door of the house. Standing on his hind legs, he gripped the doorknob in his mouth, twisted, and pulled. Then he slipped through the opening and stepped outside. The air was sharp and tangy. The sky held no moon. And snow was falling steadily.

# 21

McKinley wagged his tail with joy. The snow would cover all scents, making it hard for anyone to track Lupin.

Moving at a quick trot, he set off for Pine Smell Way and Redburn's house. Once there he stopped, studying the place. All was dark.

Lifting his head, he let loose a long, drawn-out howl, proclaiming that this was his territory and that he, McKinley, was head dog. Within moments, from all over the neighborhood, there came a satisfying response of howls, barks, and yelps. He could be sure Redburn heard that, too.

Even so, McKinley kept his eyes on the Sullivans' house. Within moments Redburn's face appeared behind a window, fogging the glass with his breath.

Lifting his leg against the Sullivans' gatepost, McKinley peed. No way that Redburn could miss this message.

As the snow continued to thicken, McKinley headed for Pycraft's house. Duchess needed to know what had happened to Lupin.

McKinley peered through the fence into Pycraft's yard. It appeared deserted, but there was enough light from the house for him to see the cable and leash system. The doghouse door was ajar, and the leash ran right into it. Duchess had to be there.

McKinley examined the fence. He blinked and cocked his head. The entryway was open. Drawing closer, he gave it a little shove. Though McKinley knew he could go on through, he held back. His ears flicked. He growled. Despite the snow, the whole area smelled of Pycraft. The stink made McKinley edgy.

He looked toward the house. Dimly, he could see the light of a flickering glow box. It meant nothing. Sometimes—McKinley didn't understand why—people left the boxes glowing all the time.

Then, for a moment, he was sure he heard the sound of another dog behind him, in the dark somewhere. He thought of Redburn. The snow should hide me, he thought. But it can hide someone else, too. He swung around. The snow worked against him. He could see or smell nothing.

Yawning with nervousness, McKinley pawed the snow and allowed himself a high-pitched growl. He made up his mind to enter the yard.

Stepping with care over one of Duchess's play sticks, McKinley trotted in, then stopped, ears up, listening. Nothing to alarm him.

He glanced back over his shoulder to make certain he could—if necessary—escape through the entryway.

When he reached the doghouse, he stuck his head

past the door. The air inside was close and damp, but full of Duchess's scent. He gave a quick, sharp bark.

"McKinley?" came the startled response. "That you?"

"It's me, all right." McKinley backed away from the door.

There was a clank as the leash banged the doghouse. Duchess crept out. "How did you get in here?"

"The entryway was open."

Duchess whimpered. "Be careful, McKinley. Pycraft may be careless, but he's mean. And he's around."

"I can take care of myself," McKinley growled.

"Why did you come?"

McKinley gazed into Duchess's eyes. "I promised you I'd help Lupin, didn't I? And I did. Aspen and I. But Lupin was wounded. We cleaned her wound and got her food. She's doing fine, now."

"Did she go back to the wilderness?"

McKinley shook his head. "She's too weak to travel. We've got her hidden."

"McKinley," Duchess whined, "the humans are

going to hunt for her this morning. Did you know that?"

"Yes. Who told you?"

"Redburn came around."

McKinley snorted.

"He spoke to me through the back fence. Said he was the new head dog. That he beat you in a fair fight. Is that true?"

"No."

"I'm really glad to hear that. Redburn was saying I should learn to make the best of my situation. That the humans were in charge of things. That it could be worse. But, McKinley, it's Lupin I'm worried about. Can you stop the hunt?"

"I'm going to try. Now listen, we've got to hurry. Do you want your collar off?"

"Oh, McKinley, could you? It's new." Duchess nodded toward Pycraft's house. "He bought it just yesterday."

McKinley growled. "I'll see what I can do."

Duchess lowered her head so he could get his teeth into the collar.

"McKinley . . . ," Duchess said.

"What?"

"You're a good dog. Thank you." Shivering in the cold, snowy air, she held as still as she could.

McKinley kept chewing. "Almost . . . a little . . . more. There! Give a shake."

Duchess shook her head. What remained of the collar fell away, dangling from the leash.

McKinley wagged his tail hard. "Come on," he barked. "Let's get out of here." He turned and froze in his tracks.

At the fence, a human was watching. "What's going on here?" came an angry voice.

"McKinley!" Duchess yelped. "It's Pycraft."

McKinley stood tall, wrinkling his nose, curling back his lips, growling.

"You again," Pycraft shouted. "What do you think you're doing?"

Baring his teeth, McKinley began to bark furiously. "Duchess! Make a bolt for it. I'll keep him busy." He advanced on the fat man, snarling.

"Steal my dog, will you!" Pycraft screamed. He

kept looking around for Duchess, who cowered off to one side. The man took a clumsy step in through the entryway, arms held wide, trying to catch her.

McKinley charged forward. Pycraft, thinking he was under attack, whirled around.

McKinley backed up.

"You stupid, meddling dog!" Pycraft spat, turning on him. "I'll teach you . . ."

"Now's your chance, Duchess!" McKinley barked. "Run for it!"

As Pycraft lunged, McKinley sidestepped and Duchess raced for the entryway.

The man staggered, saw the greyhound heading out, turned, and made a grab at her. He was too late. Duchess shot out of the yard.

McKinley, knowing it was now his time to escape, dashed forward. Pycraft spun around. Half lunging, half falling, he slammed the entryway closing shut, then latched it.

He roared at McKinley, "Let my dog go, will you?" He searched the yard and snatched up one of Duchess's play sticks. Then he moved toward McKinley, waving it in the air.

Heart pounding, McKinley snarled and snapped furiously, but backed away, wanting to stay out of reach.

As Pycraft advanced step by step, McKinley kept retreating.

The man hurled the stick.

It whipped passed McKinley's nose—almost hitting him. Recoiling sharply, he tripped over his own legs. It was then that Pycraft lunged again, using both hands to shove him into the doghouse.

McKinley felt swallowed up by darkness. Panicked, he twisted about, only to have the door of the doghouse slam shut in his face.

He was caught.

# 22

McKinley butted his head against the door. It would not budge. He scratched at it, first with one paw, then the other. It refused to give. He threw his full weight against the door. It buckled but remained firmly closed.

Furious at his predicament, McKinley howled. The sound echoed so loudly, it hurt his ears. And there was no answering call.

Shivering from fear, he smashed at the door again. Nothing gave.

Panting with exhaustion, he flopped down, rear legs tucked tightly in, front legs squashed, head bent, all at uncomfortable angles. The doghouse was much too small for him.

For a while the night was silent except for his breathing and the steady hiss of falling snow. Thinking he heard a rattle, he lifted his head, cocked his ears, and listened.

"McKinley!" came a distant bark.

"Aspen? Is that you?"

"I'm outside, at this stupid fence. But I can't get in. Where are you?"

"I'm trapped here," McKinley yowled. "In the doghouse."

"I'll try to get help."

"Aspen!"

Too late. There was no answer.

McKinley whined plaintively. If Pycraft chose to leave in the morning, there was nothing McKinley could do to stop the hunt. Or get free. At least Duchess got away, he thought. Maybe she would warn Lupin, tell her how he'd been caught.

Then McKinley remembered. He had never told the greyhound where Lupin was hiding. Besides, the snow would have covered their tracks. And, because they had come along the creek out of the hills, there would be no scent to follow. Just as he had wanted—but now, everything was all wrong.

I must be patient, McKinley thought even as he groaned with impatience. It occurred to him that if the snow kept up all night, the hunt for the wolf might be called off. But, no, people in town were used to snow. They would still go after Lupin.

Maybe the wolf was right: Better if the dogs ran off to the wilderness.

Trapped in his discomfort, McKinley thought of the pup's sleeping place. How wonderfully soft it was. And there was warmth and a feeling of safety in that house, too. He sighed. He wished he was there now. Did that mean he *was*—as Lupin claimed—a slave to humans? Or was living with them a better life?

McKinley closed his eyes. Growling and whimpering, he fell into a troubled sleep. He dreamed he was out in the open, that he was being chased. Sometimes it was Jack who was chasing him. Then

Lupin. Then Redburn. Once it was himself. Each time when he looked back, his pursuer seemed to change.

As he dreamed, his legs churned, he barked, he growled, but he did not waken.

"McKinley?"

McKinley lifted his head. Faint light outlined the doghouse doorway. It must be dawn. He listened.

"McKinley? Are you in there?" It was a human's voice. Jack's voice.

McKinley barked. A low woof answered him. Aspen was there, too.

The door to the doghouse swung open. The pup's face appeared.

"McKinley!" Jack called. "What are you doing in there, boy? Come on out here!"

Wagging his tail so hard, it banged against the side of the doghouse, McKinley scrambled into a yard deep enough in snow to reach his belly. And it was still coming down.

The boy was dressed in thick clothing, hat,

gloves, and boots. By his side stood Aspen, her face powdered with snow. She was growling with pleasure, tail wagging wildly.

McKinley leaped up on the pup, barking with joy. The boy pushed him away. "I'm really furious at you, McKinley. You wrecked my backpack. Now I can't go after the wolf. You're really a *bad* dog."

McKinley, hearing the words *backpack* and *bad* spoken so sharply, hung his head.

"And how did you get in this doghouse?" the boy demanded. "Did Mr. Pycraft put you in there? Did he? What's happening?"

McKinley barked.

Aspen chimed in with a bark of her own.

McKinley turned to her. "How'd you know I was here?"

"I saw the whole thing."

"You did? Did they start out for Lupin?"

"I think so. Pycraft isn't here. But it's still early."

"Come on, McKinley," the boy insisted. "You can't play with Aspen. We have to get home. I bet you forget you're supposed to be grounded today.

And what are you going to do about my back-pack?" He reached for McKinley's collar.

McKinley jumped back and looked up at the boy, wishing he could tell him why he'd chewed the backpack and what he still had to do. But he knew Jack wouldn't understand. Instead, wagging his tail, and with quick, short bursts, he bounded through the snow and out of the yard, Aspen by his side.

"McKinley," Jack cried. "Come back! Where you going, you bad dog?"

McKinley paused briefly to look over his shoulder. The pup was high-stepping through the snow, trying to keep up.

Aspen nudged her friend's shoulder. "The boy can wait. We need to get to Lupin."

"I hate you, McKinley!" Jack shouted tearfully. "I'm sorry I saved you. Don't ever come back! Do you hear me? Don't ever come back!"

McKinley, hearing *Don't come back* and *I hate you*, felt a stab of pain. But he pushed on, no longer looking to see if the boy was following or not.

# 23

The snowdrifts made running impossible. McKinley, with Aspen just behind, had to leap to move forward. The falling snow made it hard to see, too. Only when they reached the main ways, where early morning snowplows had already passed, was it possible to move quickly.

As they hurried along, McKinley turned to Aspen. "How did you get the pup to come for me?"

"McKinley, do you have any idea how you worry me?" she panted.

"Worry? You? Why?"

"You're always trying to take care of everything. The dogs in town. In Strawberry Park. Your humans. Duchess. Now Lupin. You make me edgy. Last night when I heard you go out, I followed."

McKinley glanced at his friend with real surprise. "I had no idea."

Aspen wagged her tail and gave a yip of amusement. "I saw you go to Redburn's house first. Then Duchess's. I watched everything that happened. I thought of jumping in, but it all happened so fast, I couldn't. Then I had to wait until Pycraft went back into his house. When he did, I tried to get the entryway open. But he had fixed it so I couldn't. That's when I barked to you. Even though you answered there was nothing I could do. I went to get Jack."

"How'd you do that?"

"For someone who takes care of so many things, you don't always notice what's around you. Do you know how often I've seen you open your house door? Enough to know how to do it. But I didn't think it would be too smart if I went in during the night. Might scare them.

"So as soon as there was a little daylight I crept

inside. Your male and female were still asleep, but it was easy enough to sniff out Jack's room. He was awake. And angry, McKinley. I think he was surprised it was me—not you. Don't you ever wish people were smarter? I do. It took a while, but he finally got the idea I needed him to follow me. Hey, why did you chew up his backpack?"

"He was going to run off with Lupin this morning. The man and woman had no idea. I couldn't figure any other way to stop the pup. I hated to leave him just now. He was really unhappy."

"You did the right thing," Aspen barked. "No saying what's going to happen. You got a plan?"

"I better check Redburn's house first. Maybe his human saw the snow and decided not to go."

"They'll go. From what I'm hearing, the humans are terribly upset about Lupin. You go ahead. I'll run back home. There's some food I can get for her. Meet you at the little house."

McKinley barked, "Great!"

"Fast as I can."

"Aspen!"

She paused and looked around.

"You're the best friend a dog ever had."

She wagged her tail, then raced away.

A few lights were on in Redburn's house. Though McKinley lifted his head and barked loudly, there was no response.

But even while he looked the lights in the house went off and the front door opened. The female Sullivan emerged and stepped into the snow. She moved toward the garage, her hand outstretched. The door began to move up. As she waited for it she saw McKinley. "McKinley!" she shouted crossly. "Get away from here!"

As soon as the garage door opened, McKinley saw that there was only one car inside. Wheeling about, he galloped down the way toward Strawberry Park.

As he ran he pondered: If the hunting party had already begun searching—and he was now sure it had—the best thing would be to keep Lupin in the cabin by the creek. With luck, Redburn would lead the hunters to the boulders where the wolf had been last seen. That would make sense. But Lupin couldn't be tracked from there. They would have to give up.

But what if somehow Redburn *did* track her to the little house? McKinley was sure the people would not go inside. Humans didn't like to share their houses with other humans, something McKinley had never understood. So everything depended upon keeping Lupin inside the cabin.

When he reached Fox Haven Way, he was happy to see it had not been plowed. And snow was still coming down. But there were new car tracks. It looked as if the people had just recently pushed through.

McKinley nosed the ruts. He could distinguish four vehicles. They had come one after the other, as if traveling in a pack. One, he was pretty sure, was Sullivan's. It was an easy track to follow.

Halfway up the way, McKinley stopped to sniff again. As he did, he heard the sound of a car behind him. He turned and stared back along the way.

A car was moving slowly toward him. Some

other hunter? As it drew closer, however, McKinley saw that on the top of car were some snow-sliding sticks.

He barked with dismay. The snow! Sliding time had arrived. Lots of humans would be coming. This car must carry the ones who used the little house. But when they opened their door, they would discover Lupin.

McKinley felt a brief moment of panic. Then— without thinking of the danger—he raced down the middle of the way toward the car, barking furiously.

He could see the man at the wheel peering out at him. But the car did not stop.

McKinley, continuing to bark, held his ground.

The man tried to swing around him. The car skidded. As the man wrenched his wheel, the rear of the car shifted sideways, finally dropping into the ditch at the edge of the way.

McKinley kept barking.

The car spun its back wheels—and sank even deeper into the ditch.

The man opened the door. "You dumb dog!" he

yelled at McKinley. "Why don't you get off the way! You think you own it?"

Two other car doors opened. Two pups emerged.

"Are we stuck, Dad?" one of them asked.

"Darned right we're stuck," the man said angrily. "Stupid dog. Has no brains. You guys get behind the car and push. I'll see if I can get us moving. Otherwise we'll have to walk to the cabin."

McKinley did not wait a moment more. With a bound he raced up the way.

When he reached the little house he found two cars and two trucks sitting in front of it. No people were around. Instead, footprints led directly into the field. McKinley lowered his head and sniffed. Redburn was with them.

Then McKinley checked to see if anyone had approached the cabin door. No prints. So far, so good.

He dashed around to the back of the house. On the snowy wood surface he crouched, then sprang at the still-open window, clearing it cleanly and landing inside.

The wolf was nowhere in sight.

"Lupin!" he barked. "Are you here?"

A low growl came from the far room.

McKinley ran to it. Lupin was stretched out on the sleeping place, her head resting on a soft lump. When McKinley came in, she looked up and around.

"Are you all right?" McKinley barked.

"Pretty well. A little stiff. There's been a lot of commotion around here. I smelled people. A dog. I tried to get out, but both door things were closed. Then things quieted down. What's happening?"

"Lots," McKinley growled. "Lupin, you can't stay anymore. The humans who live here are right down the way. They'll be arriving soon. And what you heard and smelled before was a hunting party. They're searching for you up in the hills."

Moving stiffly, Lupin crawled off the sleeping place.

"Follow me," McKinley barked. "See this here?

Soon as I open it, go. Stick close to me. How fast can you move?"

"Where are we heading?"

"Ready or not, you're going to have to start back to the wilderness. We'll take the stream again."

"Where's Aspen?" Lupin whined. "Where's Duchess?"

"Aspen's on her way. I freed Duchess, but I have no idea where she is. Hiding, I hope. Lupin, we really have to go."

Lupin refused to move. "I only spoke to a few Steamboat dogs."

"Lupin," McKinley barked, "you spoke to me. I'm head dog here. I promise! I'll give the rest of them your message."

Lupin looked at him. "A real promise?"

"Can't you trust me by now?" McKinley snapped.

Lupin gazed at him with her bright eyes. "I have no choice, do I?"

"No, you don't. And if you want to stay alive, you better hurry."

McKinley turned to the rear door. He had hardly got the knob in his mouth when the front door burst open. There stood the three humans who had been in the car.

## 24

The people gawked at McKinley and Lupin.

"Dad!" one of the pups cried out. "It's wolves!"

"Lupin! Follow me!" McKinley barked as he dove for the front door between the people's legs and the snow-sliding sticks they carried. He got by easily and headed straight for the creek. But when, in the next moment, he realized that Lupin had not followed him, he wheeled about.

Too frightened to move forward, a snarling Lupin was still inside the house.

The humans backed away from the door.

"Lupin!" McKinley yelped. "Get out of there! Hurry!"

Growling nervously, the wolf plunged out the door, but in her confusion she turned in the opposite direction, away from McKinley.

He rushed back, leaped at the wolf, and nipped her neck. Feeling attacked, Lupin twisted around, growling angrily.

"Lupin," McKinley snapped. "This way!" Once more he headed for the creek.

The people held out their snow-sliding sticks to defend themselves.

Tail bristling, Lupin bared her teeth and began to snap at them.

"Ignore them!" McKinley yelped, trying to distract the humans.

The pups turned on him, swinging their snow sliders wildly. Though aware that the man was closing in on Lupin, McKinley, fearful for himself, fell back.

Suddenly, a brown blur arched through the falling snow. It was Aspen, with a package in her mouth. She leaped at the man, pushing him away.

"Lupin! Come on!" McKinley barked.

The wolf, limping badly, lumbered toward McKinley.

With a growl of success, Aspen joined them and the three splashed down into the creek. There were a few more shouts from the humans, but the sound quickly faded.

"We really have to hurry," McKinley barked, pausing only to look around and make sure that Aspen and Lupin were still behind him.

Head bowed, panting, Lupin struggled to keep up. Aspen, the package still in her mouth, stayed close to her.

After leading them upstream some distance, McKinley halted. The snow was coming down harder, making it difficult to see or to gather in smells.

He knew that if they followed the creek they would get back into the woods and hills. That was where Lupin needed to go. But that was the way the hunters had headed. If he led her the opposite direction, across Strawberry Park, they would be free of the hunters, except going south——into town. What's more, crossing the open valley meant passing any number of human dwellings. No telling what dangers they might run into.

While McKinley thought about what to do, Aspen presented Lupin with her package. The wolf sniffed at it, took it into her mouth, and tried to bite through the wrapping. With a growl she spat it out into the water. "What is that?"

"It's meat." Aspen pounced before it was washed downstream. "But it's in a package."

"What's a package?" Lupin growled.

Aspen, her tail wagging, took up the meat by one end and swung it around so McKinley could grab the other end. Together they pulled. A slab of bacon fell into the stream.

Lupin sniffed at it briefly, then bolted it down hungrily.

McKinley faced her. "Are you well enough to travel back home now?"

The wolf turned to inspect the wound on her shoulder. A scab had formed. But blood had begun to ooze out from under it. Even so, she growled, "I can move."

"Lupin," Aspen said, sighing, "there are people up there hunting for you. They probably have guns."

"Your humans," the wolf snarled. "They're so full of hatred. How can you bear to stay with them?"

A frustrated McKinley looked into her eyes. "Lupin, if you're going to stay alive, we've got to move fast."

Lupin stared up toward the hills. The falling snow framed her broad face. Her breath puffed white. Her bright eyes grew sad. She turned to McKinley. "You said you'd bring my message to the Steamboat dogs: That my pack needs dogs if we're to survive. Will you tell them that?"

"I promised, didn't I?"

"Very well, then. I'll go home."

Aspen leaned forward and licked the wolf's nose.

McKinley barked. "I think we'd better start. Once we get you by the hunting party, you'll be safe from humans. But that might not be . . ." He didn't finish. Instead, he turned to Aspen.

She looked into his eyes. "I understand."

McKinley turned back to the wolf. "Lupin, if people appear, we'll shield you. But whatever you do, don't attack. It'll only make things worse. And if we become separated, stay high on the hill and keep working your way north."

The wolf avoided McKinley's gaze. "How many humans do you think there are?"

"Not sure. And there's a dog with them."

"What dog?" Lupin growled, her lip curling.

"The same as before: Redburn."

Lupin lifted her head and shaped her mouth into a circle.

"Don't!" McKinley snapped.

Lupin lowered her head.

The snow was falling harder than ever now. It frosted their backs. It masked their faces. Their breath made foggy plumes.

"Ready?" McKinley growled softly.

No one replied.

"Then we better start."

Lupin, then Aspen, followed him upstream.

# 25

At the way, McKinley clambered out of the creek. A car came into view, its twin headlights glowing through the thick snow. It was heading for town.

He trotted back to the others. "Car," he whimpered.

Lupin raised her head to watch. "What's that?"

"You'll see," Aspen answered.

The three remained perfectly still as the car rolled by. The driver gave no indication he had noticed them.

Lupin trembled. "How does it move?"

Aspen shook her head. "I'm not sure."

McKinley grunted. "Let's go." He led them over

the way. Once on the far side he stepped back into the creek, which, on this side, had become clotted with snow. The only way to follow it was by its faint scent.

Nose down, McKinley guided the others across the field and up into the hills. Every few steps he paused, lifted his head and, ears pricked forward, listened intently. The weather, he knew, was dulling his hearing as well as his sense of smell. Though he strained for the slightest whiff of the humans or Redburn, he detected nothing. There was no choice but to keep moving.

After a few moments he stopped again and looked back. Lupin's limp was becoming more pronounced. Aspen was following right behind her. When Lupin moved, she moved. When she stopped, so did Aspen. McKinley, watching, saw his friend occasionally give Lupin a little nudge whenever she faltered.

They pushed on, traveling slowly but steadily. Suddenly, McKinley stopped. He lifted his nose and sniffed. A low growl rose in his chest.

Aspen drew close. "What is it?"

McKinley cocked his head and flicked his ears forward. "I'm not sure."

Lupin snapped, "Humans?" Her eyes were half lidded with encrusted snow.

McKinley sighed. "I think so. They're off that way." He pointed with his nose to show her. "If we keep following the creek, we'll be heading right toward them. We have to go a different way."

"But if we leave the water," Lupin whined, "won't it be easier for that dog to follow us?"

Aspen stepped forward. "Lupin, I think McKinley is saying we don't have a choice."

McKinley shifted uneasily. "The snow will help hide us." For the first time, he heard Lupin whimper. He tried to ignore it. "There's a ridge in front of us. Along the top is a line of sticks stuck in the ground. I've been with my pup lots of times when we've come upon them. He told me there was no hunting beyond those markers."

"Who's your pup?" Lupin growled.

"My young human. The one with me the first time we met."

"I met him before I met you. He was full of fear."

"Lupin," McKinley snapped, "that boy wants to join your pack. I think he wants to be a wolf."

Lupin gazed into McKinley's eyes. "I don't understand your world."

"It *is* hard to understand."

The wolf made no further sound.

Aspen gave her a gentle nudge. "Please. Let's go."

Snowdrifts had formed. McKinley broke through them with his broad chest to make passage easier for the others.

They soon reached a clump of trees at the edge of a rise. Here the snow was less deep. But there were more bushes. McKinley had to slow their pace.

Suddenly he caught a scent and stopped. Even as he did, barking erupted from beyond the bushes. A call to attention.

"It's Redburn," McKinley snarled. "He's not far away. Sounds like he's caught a whiff of us."

Lupin panted, "Where are the people?"

McKinley took a deep sniff, turning his head. "They're spread out from there to there on either side of Redburn. Like a thin moon coming toward us." Then, with a growl, he snapped, "I can smell guns. Come on."

Though still heading uphill, he set off in a different direction.

Lupin groaned at the faster pace. "McKinley!"

"What?"

"I can't go so fast."

"You have to."

Aspen drew closer to the wolf. "I'll help." She pushed at Lupin from the rear.

They continued on for a few paces.

Lupin stopped. "No more," she whimpered in pain. "I'd rather stand and fight." The caked snow on her wound had turned pink.

McKinley gazed at her for a moment. Then he looked at Aspen. "Take the lead. I'll guard the rear. Whatever happens, don't worry about me. Keep heading uphill. Don't stop until you reach a marker."

"I'm not afraid to fight them," Lupin snarled angrily.

McKinley drew so close, the wolf's breath mingled with his. "Lupin, if you fight, you'll lose. I won't let them kill you."

"Why should you care?"

"We need you."

Lupin shook her head, tossing the snow away from her eyes and staring hard at McKinley. "Need me? What for?"

McKinley turned away from the wolf's gaze. He became aware of his own beating heart, and the gentle but unceasing sound of the falling snow all around him. The snow was so light—like summer dust—but branches bowed under its weight.

Lupin shifted her body nervously. "Answer my question!"

McKinley faced the wolf. "Lupin, you remind me of what we dogs once were. What I could be."

He heard Aspen gasp.

"Does that mean you might still join us?" Lupin snapped.

McKinley, not answering, turned away.

Lupin gazed at McKinley for a long moment. Then she faced the hunters. "How close are they?" she asked.

McKinley turned back. "Not far."

For a moment the wolf held still. Then she sighed. "Very well. I'll try to escape."

Aspen trotted forward. As she passed McKinley, she paused to touch his nose with hers. Then she opened her mouth wide and gently nipped his muzzle. He gave her a lick across her nose. Eyes averted, he moved toward the rear, pausing when he drew even with Lupin.

"Aspen will get you there," he panted into the wolf's ear. "Don't give up."

Her face shrouded again by snow, Lupin turned sad eyes on him. Slowly, she bowed her head. "McKinley," she whimpered, "you are a true head dog. I, who am a free wolf, honor you."

McKinley shook his head with impatience. "Let's see what happens."

Aspen nudged the wolf. "We need to go."

As they moved off—at a slower pace now—McKinley let himself trail farther and farther behind. It was not long before the falling snow seemed to swallow them whole.

Once the two were out of sight, McKinley halted. Lupin and Aspen would have to make their own way.

For a moment he closed his eyes. To whom, he asked himself, did he owe his loyalty? To the dog pack, to his humans, to wolves, or . . . to himself?

He turned and looked toward Redburn and the humans—with their guns. As he stood there, McKinley wondered how much—in the snow—he might look like a wolf.

# 26

From somewhere in the snowy deep came the sound of twigs crackling.

Then barking erupted. McKinley cocked his head. He knew it was Redburn, gloating.

Oaf, McKinley thought.

The barking came again.

McKinley's senses told him that the setter was farther up the hill. He lifted his nose to catch the drift of the air, determining quickly that he was almost downwind of him. Shifting so that the air-flow came directly his way, he inhaled deeply. The hunting party was drawing closer.

Redburn barked again.

McKinley understood the barks as the sound of an excited, very confident dog.

He began to trot up the hill right toward the barks. Feeling sure of himself, he broke into a run. Faster and faster he went, his heart pounding in time with his thumping feet.

With his head well-forward, tail stuck straight out behind him, McKinley lengthened his strides more and more. No longer did he care how much noise he made. Instead, he smashed through bushes and breasted through snowdrifts. Never had he felt so strong.

Redburn was baying with triumph, high-stepping grandly through the snow, head erect, nose up, when McKinley spotted him.

When McKinley drew near enough, he launched himself into the air, forelegs extended. Before the setter knew he was even being attacked, McKinley hit him broadside.

Taken completely by surprise, Redburn went tumbling. With a yelp of shock and fright, he struggled to get back on his legs.

McKinley, landing on the setter's far side, spun about, then flung himself at the dog again. Once more the setter fell, once more he went wallowing desperately in the snow.

McKinley leaped yet again, landing with his four feet on top of Redburn. Bending down, he nipped the setter's neck with enough force to make the dog cry out.

"Pet! Dogcatcher!" McKinley snarled. "Catch me if you can!"

The next instant he broke away, charging uphill in a direction opposite from Aspen and Lupin's.

Behind him he heard Redburn howling with fury. The next moment he caught the panting, thudding sounds of the setter coming after him. It was exactly what he wanted.

Sure enough, the next moment he heard a shout, Sullivan's voice: "Redburn's got the wolf on the run! I see him! Follow him!"

Whooping with excitement, the humans began to run, too.

McKinley sprinted uphill. When he reached the

crest, he paused to listen. Redburn, barking madly, was pressing hard after him. The humans were racing right along.

I must confuse them, McKinley thought. If I can lead them back to where they started, the trail will be so muddled, Redburn will never be able to lead the humans to Lupin.

But where did they begin? McKinley asked himself. The next moment he was sure he knew: the boulders.

With a series of loud barks, he sped almost straight down the hill. Slipping and sliding, he made a terrible racket. He didn't care at all. The more noise he made, the more certain he was that he would be followed.

Sure enough, he heard Redburn coming after him, yapping at the top of his lungs. The excited humans shouted in pursuit.

McKinley plunged on.

Only when he saw the boulders did he slow down. Panting with exertion, tongue lolling, he skirted Duchess's hideaway and burst into the clearing.

There stood Pycraft, a long gun in his hands.

# 27

McKinley skidded to a stop. He and the human stared at each other.

His hair bristling, a low growl thundering in his chest, McKinley hunkered down. He curled his lips to reveal his teeth.

"You!" Pycraft yelled. "You're not a dog. You're a wolf!"

McKinley slowly rose and snarling, began to move toward the man.

"Back off!" Pycraft yelled. "Attack me, and I'll shoot. Do you hear me, you fool animal! I mean it. I'm warning you, I'll show you who's in charge." He aimed his long gun right at McKinley.

McKinley saw the man's hand tighten.

It was then, from behind the boulders, that Jack appeared. Screaming, he dove for Pycraft's legs, tumbling him.

Thrown off balance, the man jerked his gun upward and fired. The shot whipped over McKinley's head.

As Jack worked to free himself, McKinley leaped at Pycraft, his forepaws hard on the man's chest. The gun flew beyond reach.

"Help! Help!" Pycraft cried. "I'm being attacked by the wolf!"

As the man tried to scramble away, McKinley snatched the gun out of the snow. Dragging it with his teeth, he tore down the hill. He heard his pup trying to follow.

"Hurry! Hurry!" Pycraft screamed. "The wolf's got my rifle."

Halfway downhill, McKinley stopped and dropped the gun. Frantically, he dug a pit in the snow, pushed the gun into it, then used his back legs to heap snow over it. By the time he was done, Jack had caught up with him.

"Are you all right, boy?" the pup asked breathlessly.

McKinley leaped with happiness at Jack, covering the pup's face with licks.

"McKinley," Jack cried, laughing. "Stop! What are you doing? Come on, guy. Get off."

McKinley stepped back.

"McKinley," the boy said, a grin on his face, "first you get locked in Mr. Pycraft's doghouse. Then you're about to get yourself killed. How many times do I have to save you? I mean, what is going on?"

McKinley studied the pup's face, trying to understand his words.

"You think you're so smart. When you ran off with Aspen, I just followed your footprints. I figured you were getting involved in that wolf hunt. I mean, there were dog prints from that cabin right up to those boulders, so I knew exactly where you went. But when I got up here, all I saw was Mr. Pycraft with his rifle. I figured he was waiting for the wolf. When he didn't see me, I hid. Good thing I did, boy, wasn't it? You know what? I think he thought *you* were the wolf. He was going to shoot you. What did you do with the gun?"

McKinley, hearing the word *gun,* scratched at the snow, until Jack saw the butt end.

"Oh man, McKinley," he exclaimed, "you *are* so smart." He shoved the snow back, then tramped it down. "Guess they won't find that sucker till next May."

McKinley, suddenly remembering that Jack was supposed to be in his gathering place, took a few steps down the hill, looked around, barked, then whined impatiently.

Jack looked back up the hill. "Wait a minute. McKinley, were you helping the wolf get away? Is *that* what this is all about?"

The *wolf* word. McKinley cocked his head and gazed at the pup. Did Jack understand?

The boy threw himself down on his knees and

hugged the dog hard. "Man, McKinley, if you did, I'm so glad. I really am."

McKinley, trying to get the boy to move, pranced off.

"Yeah, let's get out of here. You know, McKinley, for chewing my backpack and all, I really should be mad at you. But if you helped that wolf get away, I'll forgive you."

McKinley, understanding *mad,* looked around. When he saw the pup didn't look mad, he trotted on.

Suddenly, as though from a great distance, he heard a long, drawn-out howl, a howl free and triumphant. McKinley stopped and turned uphill. A shiver ran down his back.

Jack stopped, too. "McKinley," he cried. "That's the wolf! Did you hear it? He did get away! Dang, that's so beautiful, isn't it? Hey, boy, don't you wish you could howl like that?"

McKinley stared up into the falling snow. The cold flakes touched his warm eyes and made them tear up.

\* \* \*

After making sure the boy got to his gathering place, McKinley headed home. Snow was still falling lightly when he reached his newly cleared way. A snowplow was just turning the corner.

As he neared his house, Duchess came scrambling out of the bushes. "McKinley!" she barked.

McKinley stopped.

"Where's Lupin?"

McKinley looked briefly over his shoulder. "She's safe and pretty much away."

"I was so worried," Duchess whined, sounding apologetic. "But I didn't know where to go. You never told me where she was. So I hid. What's happened?"

When the story was done, Duchess barked excitedly. "I'm leaving, McKinley. I'm going to join Lupin's wolf pack."

"Good girl. Do you know where to find her?"

"Up in the Zirkel Wilderness," she said. "It's a huge area, but I think I'll be able to sniff her out."

McKinley sat. "If you still want my advice, go

now. And go through town. That way you won't meet any of those hunters. Or Pycraft. Lupin should be moving slowly. With your speed, you should catch up with her easily."

"Thanks." Duchess started off. After a few paces she stopped and turned back. "McKinley, what's going to happen to you?"

McKinley barked. "Me? I'll be fine."

"Are you sure? This morning, early, before Redburn went off looking for the wolf, he set up a meeting of the pack. See, I was hiding in some bushes over by Cat Litter Way. I heard Luna tell Star about that meeting. I guess Redburn's claiming that he's head dog now."

"Is he?"

"That's why he called that meeting for tonight. On Howl Hill. Regular time."

McKinley barked, "Guess he thought he was going to catch Lupin. Hey, I'm not letting it worry me. Any dog in the pack is free to call a meeting."

"McKinley . . . well, you don't need suggestions from me. And I better go. Thanks . . ." The greyhound lifted a paw, then, without waiting for a wag of McKinley's tail, she raced down the way.

McKinley watched her go, tail drooping. "A pack meeting," he whimpered. With a shake of his head he turned toward his door and opened it.

It was still morning, but he was exhausted. He had taken care of everything: Lupin, Duchess, the boy. Now he had only a couple of more things to do: go to that meeting Redburn had called and deliver Lupin's message to the pack.

# 28

McKinley stood still, enjoying the warmth and familiar smells inside his house.

The female was in the kitchen staring at some pieces of paper and eating.

When McKinley came in, she looked around. "McKinley! You bad dog. You were supposed to stay in all day. You should be ashamed of yourself."

The man came into the room. He seemed ready to leave. "Look who's not been here. And filthy, too!"

McKinley, worried by the words *bad, stay,* and *filthy,* and wanting to reassure them, drew close to the female, sat up, and put a paw on her lap.

She fondled it—even as she kept it from marking her body covering. "Oh, well," she said, "he's probably forgotten what he's done."

"Might have been pot roast to us, but it was just food to him." The man laughed and rubbed McKinley behind his ears.

Happy to have cheered them up, McKinley gave a bark of pleasure, then checked his food bowl. It was full. He ate, then padded down to the pup's room, leaped onto the sleeping place and, with his head on Jack's lump of softness, fell asleep.

A bark from Aspen woke him.

Startled, McKinley opened his eyes. She was standing right next to his sleeping place. "Are you all right?"

"Oh, sure."

"Where's Lupin?"

"I left her way past the markers. She was limping but heading home. She's tough, McKinley.

She'll make it. What did you do to keep Redburn away?"

McKinley told how he had tricked the setter and how Jack had saved him from being shot. "And, in the end, Duchess decided to go after Lupin."

"Good for her!" Aspen barked. "How are you feeling?"

"I'm fine." McKinley suddenly sat up. "Hey, how did you get in here?"

Aspen wagged her tail. "It's midday. All your people are gone. I let myself in. McKinley, you're lucky your pup was there."

"I know." McKinley flopped down again. "Aspen, Redburn has called a pack meeting."

"When's it happening?"

"Tonight. Out on Howl Hill."

"What's it about?"

"He thinks he deserves to be head dog."

"McKinley, the pack would never choose Redburn."

McKinley rested his head on his front paws. "You know what? Sometimes I wish they would. That way, you'd get your wish."

"What's that?"

"Didn't you tell me I should stop taking care of everyone?"

Aspen sighed. "You better get some more sleep."

McKinley looked up, licked her nose, and wagged his tail. "I will." With that, he closed his eyes and drifted off to sleep again.

When he woke, Jack was beside him, lying on his stomach, head propped in his hands.

McKinley, wagging his tail, looked at the boy.

Jack rumpled McKinley's ears. "Guess what, McKinley? The wolf got away. I went downtown after school. That's all people are talking about. So if that's what you were trying to do, you sure did it."

McKinley gazed at the pup, then licked his face.

Jack laughed. "Just as well, I guess. I have to admit, with all this snow it wouldn't have been smart for me to have gone off with him. You going to tell me you made the snow happen, too?"

McKinley wagged his tail.

"Hey," said Jack, "you know what? I'm starving. Want something to eat?"

McKinley, watching the pup head for the food place, thought of how much he wanted to thank him for saving his life. But a lick on the face wouldn't be enough this time.

## 29

For the rest of the afternoon, McKinley slept. And when, that early evening, his humans gathered to watch the glow box, he was content to curl up and sleep some more.

When McKinley finally woke—fully rested—the house was dark, and the people had all gone to sleep.

He went to a window and looked out, checking the position of the moon. It was time.

He padded into Jack's room. He leaped onto the soft sleeping place and licked the boy's face.

Jack, slow to wake, mumbled, "McKinley, you dope, it's Saturday. I don't have to go to school."

McKinley persisted.

"What is it, boy?" Jack asked. "What's the matter?"

Taking a gentle grip on the pup's hand, McKinley pulled.

The sleepy boy sat up, rubbed his eyes, and glanced at his small buzz box. "Dang, McKinley! Are you nuts? It's two o'clock in the morning. What's the matter? Is something wrong?"

McKinley gave a soft yelp, wagged his tail, went to the door, then came back to the soft sleeping place.

"What are you trying to tell me, boy? Has something happened? Is there a fire? Is the wolf back? Are Mom and Dad okay?"

McKinley picked up Jack's shoes and dropped them at the boy's feet. Then he dragged over the things the pup put on his body.

Jack stared at him. "You want me to get dressed, boy? Is that it?"

McKinley looked up at the pup's face, wagged his tail vigorously, and whined with impatience.

"Okay, McKinley. But I'm telling you, this better be important. It really better be."

As soon as Jack was ready, McKinley led him to the front door and then opened it.

"So neat that Mom taught you to do that," Jack said with a grin.

McKinley wagged his tail, stepped outside, looked back at the boy, and whined.

"Have you gone crazy, McKinley?" Jack said in a hushed voice. "You wanting me to go out in the middle of the night? What is bugging you?"

McKinley growled, frisked away, and looked back.

"Okay, I get it: You want me to come with you." The pup fetched more body covering as well as something for his head and hands.

As Jack came back outside, he said, "McKinley, you are one weird dog. You just better know what you're doing."

McKinley led the pup through the quiet town. The sky was clear, speckled with stars and the bright light of the glowing moon, which cast a glow over everything. The air was cold but calm.

"Hey, McKinley," Jack said as they walked along.

"I forgot to tell you. Guess what happened to Mr. Pycraft?"

McKinley, hearing the word *Pycraft,* stopped and looked up at his pup.

"My dad told me he didn't even have a license for his gun. And that dog of his, Duchess, guess what? She ran away again."

McKinley, understanding *Pycraft, gun,* and *Duchess,* studied Jack's face.

"So we did a good thing, buddy. A good thing!"

McKinley, content with the word *good,* moved on.

As they continued through town, dogs began to emerge from their houses. Most came alone. But there were pairs and a few trios. There were pups, big-footed and frolicsome, who had to be reminded—sometimes with a nod or a nip— that this was a solemn occasion. There were young dogs, sleek and alert, ears pricked forward, as though ready for anything—even a bit of a fight. There were old dogs, grizzled and watery-eyed, who plodded along slowly, heads bobbing with every step. They were all walking softly in the same direction McKinley and Jack were headed.

When the dogs saw McKinley, some nodded, but there was no attempt at communication. For the most part, eyes were cast down.

McKinley wondered how many of them had heard directly from Redburn.

"McKinley," Jack asked in a nervous, low voice, "what's going on? How come all these dogs are out? There must be hundreds. Where are we going?"

McKinley looked reassuringly up at the boy and wagged his tail, but kept quiet.

The procession moved across the river bridge, then passed the place where people rode horses and bulls. It circled around the fields where—in the hot season—the pups hit balls with sticks. Next they passed the building where people with snow-sliders gathered. Finally, they reached the area the dogs called Howl Hill. Here a noisy machine pulled people to the top of the hill, from which they rushed down or jumped in the air on snow-sliders.

As they approached, Jack leaned over and said, "McKinley, that sign says, 'No Dogs in Ski Areas.'"

Paying no attention, McKinley kept going.

Jack, looking around warily at the growing numbers of gathering dogs, stayed close, now and again reaching down and touching McKinley's head.

When they reached the foot of the hill, McKinley sat down in the midst of the other dogs. Jack, at his side, sat, too. Not long after, Aspen joined them.

"Hey, Aspen," Jack cried, "how you doing, girl? Hey, McKinley, even your girlfriend's here."

McKinley turned, and he and Aspen touched noses.

She whimpered. "What do you think will happen?"

McKinley shook his head.

## 30

McKinley took in the scene around him: The snowy slope illuminated by moonlight; all of the town's dogs waiting quietly at the bottom. He saw them steal looks at him. Occasionally a growl erupted, even a snarl. Mostly, however, tails were wagging. There was only an infrequent bark. But ears were tilted forward; tongues lolled from open mouths. Here and there a leg scratched earnestly.

"Are these all the dogs in town, McKinley?" Jack whispered. "Do you guys do this a lot?" he asked.

McKinley, wishing to reassure the pup, simply

licked his face. Then he turned back to study the pack again, trying to gauge their mood. He knew them all, could have named each one. There was Gibby. And there was Barkley. Jacque, Brittany, and Hunter were sitting calmly. Star, too. Max, Pepper, Tubbs, and Duke had begun fooling around. Jayvee was scratching her ever-present fleas. Buster was asleep.

But McKinley was also searching the pack for Redburn and his friends, Boots and Jaws. When he caught sight of them, the three were huddled together in the middle of the crowd. But even as McKinley watched, Redburn broke away and started to climb the hill, his two friends staying close to his heels.

Redburn stopped halfway up the hill, faced the dogs below, and sat.

Jack leaned over to McKinley. "That's Redburn, isn't it?" he asked. "The Sullivans' dog. I heard he was hunting the wolf. Is he the dogs' boss?"

McKinley kept his eyes on the big setter.

Redburn stood. As always, his fur looked perfectly

burnished. He held his head high, his tail extended. His leg feathers fluttered gracefully. McKinley had to admit he looked good.

Ears pitched forward, eyes wide open and bright, Redburn pointed his nose at the moon, opened his mouth, and barked. "I, Redburn, hereby call to order a full meeting of the Steamboat pack, as is the right of every dog."

The mass of dogs arrayed below lifted their heads and returned Redburn's cry with a chorus of howling, yowling, and baying. "We are here! We are here! We Steamboat dogs are here," they returned. "Let the meeting begin."

"McKinley," Jack whispered nervously, "what's happening? What are they saying?"

McKinley, with eyes and ears only for Redburn, ignored the pup.

"Steamboat dogs," the setter went on, "I called this meeting because we all have been placed in serious jeopardy. McKinley allowed a savage wolf to come among us. By doing so he defied our humans' wishes. McKinley has endangered us by making the humans think of us as uncivilized beasts!

"Steamboat dogs, our humans feed us, shelter us," Redburn barked excitedly. "In return, we must do what they want. That's the way we should live. In complete obedience. It's the civilized way.

"And that's why I called this meeting. I, Redburn, among all Steamboat dogs, have the greatest trust of the humans. Because they admire me so much, you should make *me* head dog."

Boots and Jaws lifted their heads and barked their noisy approval.

In response, other dogs barked and howled. "Answer him, McKinley! Answer Redburn's charges!"

McKinley, still sitting, looked around. He barked briskly once, twice.

The dogs instantly hushed themselves.

Up on the hill, Redburn tossed his head importantly, but sat down.

"Steamboat dogs," McKinley began from his place, "Redburn is right: We were visited by a wolf. Lupin is her name. She came down to us from the Zirkel Wilderness. Her mission was to bring dogs back to her home so they could help increase her diminishing wolf pack.

"She may have been a stranger, but Steamboat dogs, she is our kin. These wolves are what we once were. If for no other reason, we owe wolves our respect, our courtesy.

"As for this Lupin, she is more powerful than me. She is so strong that I bowed before her."

There was an eruption of growls, barks, and whimpers from the dogs.

"See, see!" Redburn barked excitedly. "McKinley bowed before the wolf. He gave away his leadership! I'd never do such a thing. It's I who should be our leader!"

"But I must also tell you," McKinley continued, his barks rising above Redburn's, "that this Lupin was nearly caught by some humans—led by a dog. The humans would have killed this kin of ours if they could. But even though the wolf was wounded, she managed to escape.

"Steamboat dogs, listen to me. There is one dog among us who helped the humans hunt Duchess, an abused dog—as some of you know. Duchess only wanted her freedom. In seeking to free her, Lupin came to be wounded. Shot by a long gun. And when she was bleeding, that same dog tried to hunt her down again. The dog who did all this was—Redburn."

At the mention of his name, Redburn began to bark furiously. "Steamboat dogs, listen! McKinley gave up his authority. To a stranger. You heard him admit it. By bowing to this wolf he went against what's best for us! We need stronger leadership."

Most dogs on the hill began to bark and bay at him, "Traitor. Turncoat! Lapdog! Pet!"

The setter barked more fiercely than ever. "No, you're not paying attention! I should be the pack leader. I'd never give way to a wolf."

There was an uproar of barks. Jack reached for McKinley, who glanced at him and saw fear in his eyes.

"Curs!" Redburn snapped at the dogs. "Mutts! Mongrels! Listen to your better!"

At these taunts the dogs, on their feet now, only increased their yowls.

McKinley watched tensely as some of the dogs began to move up the hill. At first Redburn stood his ground and only barked at them furiously. But as more dogs began to close in, he and his friends started to back away.

Suddenly, McKinley stood, his paws braced wide on the snowy ground. His chest seemed to expand with strength. His great tail curved over his broad, black back, the fur of which had risen with tension. Then he opened his mouth wide and exposed his teeth, too, wrinkling his nose to do so. From his chest he let forth a deep, rumbling growl.

Instantly, the other dogs hushed. Those inching up the hill halted. Even Redburn shut his mouth and paid attention.

"Steamboat dogs," McKinley barked into the deep silence, "I say that Redburn is a dog who does whatever humans tell him instead of honoring the best interests of our pack. Or of any needful dog. Redburn is a leash-licker! A groveler. A slave to every human whim, willing to crawl into the lap of any human who offers to pat him on the head. Yes, Redburn is a dog, but he is without a dog's dignity."

The assembled dogs began to growl angrily. "Bad dog!" they yapped at Redburn. "Bad dog! You should be ashamed of yourself. Bad dog!"

Those dogs on the hill began to advance again, snarling and yapping. Others joined them to surround the setter.

While the tumult grew and the dogs edged closer, Redburn seemed to shrink in size. He made an effort to lift his head as if to protest, snapping this way and that. Then, as even more dogs crowded up the hill, he, Jaws, and Boots began to retreat.

The dog closest to Redburn darted forward, growling loudly, teeth bared.

Whimpering, Boots and Jaws bolted, leaving Redburn alone.

"All I am trying to explain . . . ," the setter whined.

Another dog darted forward, making clicking sounds with his teeth.

"Steamboat dogs!" McKinley suddenly barked. "Don't demean yourself by fighting with such a dog. Don't treat Redburn the way he wished to treat the wolf. He isn't worth it. Let him go!"

The advancing dogs, their mouths open, tongues lolling, halted in their tracks.

Redburn looked around sheepishly. He was surrounded. Skulking down, he dropped his tail between his legs. Whimpering, he began to slink off the hill. As he descended, the pack made way for him, growling and snapping at him as he passed.

At the bottom of the hill, Redburn turned briefly. For a moment McKinley thought he was about to bark something, but the setter seemed to have second thoughts. With a yelp, he scampered away.

Once Redburn was gone, the dogs turned their attention back to McKinley. "Take your place!" they cried at him. "Up on the hill, where you belong."

McKinley took a step forward but paused to put his mouth around one of Jack's gloved hands and pull at him.

"I'm coming, McKinley," he said. "I'm coming."

McKinley and the pup made their way up the hill, to the same spot Redburn had taken. There McKinley paused. After making sure Jack sat, he turned to face the dogs who were now below him.

"Steamboat dogs," McKinley said, "I promised to bring you the wolf's message. Listen to what Lupin wanted you to hear.

"She asked me if we dared to live without humans caring for us, if we dared to be completely free. She challenged me to imagine what it would mean to our lives if our pups were not taken away from us but remained by our sides for all our days. She asked if we had the courage to live and die by the use of our own muscles and brains. Could we live in a world larger, wilder than ours is now? By doing so she reminded me that we dogs are descendants of wolves, and that there is still some wolf within each of us.

"Steamboat dogs, Duchess has already gone over to the wolves. All of you are free to join Lupin's wolf pack in the Zirkel Wilderness. You will be welcomed.

"That is the message Lupin brought and which I promised to give you. Whether you go or not is your decision to make."

There were barks of, "What do you think, McKinley? Give us your thoughts. What shall you do?"

"Steamboat dogs," McKinley replied, "since you ask my opinion, I'll give it. I answer: Yes, we *are* decedents of wolves. Let us be proud of that. But we are still *dogs.* We care for our humans. They need us to protect them, to care for their pups. In turn, they take care of us, providing food and shelter.

"That does not mean we must be their slaves or do everything they ask of us. Not at all. If we are to remain their friends we must be their equals. We must be equals so that through living together each kind may be different."

McKinley, turning to Jack, nudged him, encouraging him to stand up.

"Here is an example of what I'm telling you," McKinley barked to the dogs. "Look on this pup. His name is Jack. He is my human pup. I raised him from the time he was helpless. I guarded him. Watched over him. Kept him safe. Now he is almost grown.

"Yesterday, in the early morning, he saved me from a man who first wished to cage me and then wanted to kill me. Without this boy I would not have been able to free the wolf. Nor would I have lived.

"Steamboat dogs! I call upon you to recognize this human pup for the friend he is! Let this boy be voted an honorary dog!"

As one, the mass of dogs lifted their heads and bayed their loud approval.

Then McKinley rose up on his rear legs, rested his forepaws on Jack's shoulders, and licked the pup's nose.

A grinning Jack, even as he hugged McKinley,

said, "What are they saying, McKinley? What are they doing?"

McKinley dropped down and began to trot off the hill.

Suddenly Aspen stood up. "Steamboat dogs," she bayed, "there's one more thing to do."

The pack, turning to face her, hushed themselves.

McKinley, with Jack at his side, halted.

"Redburn," Aspen continued, "called this meeting so you would choose him to be head dog. He's gone. But what about McKinley? Do you wish him to remain our leader? I know him well. He won't request it, but he needs your reassurance. Steamboat dogs, let him hear your will. Is McKinley still to be our head dog?"

As one, the dogs leaped to their feet, howled, barked, and yapped yes yes yes! wagging their tails so hard, they whipped the snow into a cloud.

"Steamboat dogs," McKinley barked over all the noise, his tail wagging, too, "thank you. You do me a great honor."

Then he lifted his head high, shaped his mouth

in an almost perfect circle, and began to howl. Remembering Lupin's cry, he let forth a howl that was part moan, part cry of triumph, throaty and rough-edged at first. It rose to a single clear note that vaulted as high as the sky, and down over the dogs before him, then out along the whole valley.

The dogs—as well as Jack—grew silent and listened in awe . . . for all who heard that howl felt their hearts awaken.

# 31

McKinley and Aspen walked home side by side. Jack meandered along with them. "McKinley, boy," the pup said, "that was so cool. I just wish I knew what it was all about. Thanks for letting me come. And that howl you did, man, it was something else."

Aspen suddenly turned to McKinley. "Why did you care so much about what happens to Lupin?"

McKinley plodded along for a while in silence. "I'm not sure. Maybe because she's free."

"Aren't we?"

McKinley shook his head. "Remember how she

talked about the wilderness? It sounded so wonderful. But then, look at the boy. He doesn't know what happened. Still, he's pretty wonderful, too. And then there's you, Aspen. What you just did. And this town—it's great to be here." He wagged his tail.

Aspen wagged back.

Reaching home, McKinley stopped and gave her a nuzzle. "Good night. And . . . thank you." The two dogs touched noses.

"You're always going to take care of everything, anyway, aren't you?"

"I like to."

"You do it well, too. Good night, head dog." Aspen, tail wagging, headed for her own house.

"Come on, buddy," Jack called as he pushed open their door. Once inside, he stamped his feet free of snow while McKinley shook himself, spattering snow everywhere. Then both went into the large room. The man and woman were there.

"Hey!" Gil demanded angrily. "Where have you guys been?"

"Have you any idea what time it is?" Sarah asked.

As Jack began to talk, McKinley went to his water bowl, lapped up some water, then went on to Jack's room. He jumped on the sleeping place and lay down, his head on the soft lump. He could hear the murmur of voices down the hall.

After a while Jack came into the room. "McKinley!" he cried. "You got paw prints all over the bed!"

But the pup didn't seem to mind, really. Instead, he pulled off his body coverings and got in his sleeping place next to McKinley, drawing a cloth over both of them. He didn't bother to turn off the light.

The pup looked into McKinley's face. "McKinley," he said, "guess what? They didn't believe me when I told them where we were. I tried to explain how all you dogs got together and barked. You know what they said? Said I was making it up. Dreaming.

"And another thing. Up on the hill. That howl you gave. You never did that before. I loved it. Can you do it again?"

McKinley gazed at the pup, and licked his nose again.

The boy sighed. "Good thing it's still Saturday, boy. We can sleep in." He was silent. Then: "McKinley, guess what? I've figured out what I'm going to do when I grow up."

McKinley, wondering what the boy was saying, studied him closely.

"I'm going learn how to talk to you," the boy went on. "And how you can talk to me. Get it? A dog scientist. That would be so cool, wouldn't it? Bet I'd be famous if I did. You, too." He reached out and gave McKinley a hug. "But do you know what else?" Jack added.

McKinley, ears cocked, stared at the boy.

"I just wish I knew what you were thinking right now." The boy rolled over and gave McKinley another hug, and a kiss on his snout.

As Jack fell into a deep sleep, McKinley wondered what in the world the boy had been talking about so seriously. He gave Jack yet another lick across the nose. In his sleep, the boy smiled.

McKinley knew that, among humans, a smile meant the same as a wagging tail.

He closed his eyes. As he did, the image of Lupin filled his mind. He saw her slowly making her way through the dark night with only Duchess and stars as her companions. She was limping, yet moving steadily over the cold snow, journeying toward her home in the wilderness.

McKinley wondered if any other dogs from the Steamboat pack would follow her. He found himself hoping some would. For a moment he even felt his own blood stir, his legs churn slightly. Then, with a sigh that was equal parts regret, pride, and weariness, McKinley slept the sleep of a good dog.

**"Kids who get called the worst names oftentimes find each other. That's how it was with us."**

Skeezie, Addie, Joe, and Bobby are by no means the popular kids at school. But they have been friends forever. And if you really want to survive middle school, that's all it takes.

★"A fast, funny, tender story that will touch readers."
—*Booklist*, starred review

"A knock-out, one of the best of the year."
—*San Francisco Chronicle*

A Book Sense 76 Top Ten Selection

★"This narrator is anything but an average Joe: [He's] candid, memorable, and—though he might find this hard to believe— totally charismatic."
—*Publishers Weekly*, starred review

Listen up for Addie's side of the story in *Addie on the Inside*, coming May 2011

# MIDDLE-GRADE ADVENTURES FROM
## THREE-TIME NEWBERY HONOR–WINNING AUTHOR
# Zilpha Keatley Snyder

William S. and
the Great Escape

The Egypt Game

The Headless Cupid

The Witches of Worm

The Bronze Pen

The Treasures
of Weatherby

From Atheneum Books for Young Readers
Published by Simon & Schuster

# How many of these award-winning books have you read?

THE UNDERNEATH
by Kathi Appelt

THE EGYPT GAME
by Zilpha Keatley Snyder

THE HEADLESS CUPID
by Zilpha Keatley Snyder

THE WITCHES OF WORM
by Zilpha Keatley Snyder

THE HOUSE OF THE SCORPION
by Nancy Farmer

SHADOW OF A BULL
By Maia Wojciechowska

JENNIFER, HECATE, MACBETH,
WILLIAM MCKINLEY AND ME,
ELIZABETH
by E. L. Konigsburg

THE TOMBS OF ATUAN
by Ursula K. Le Guin

THE COURAGE OF SARAH NOBLE
by Alice Dalgliesh

ONE-EYED CAT
by Paula Fox

HATCHET
by Gary Paulsen

DOGSONG
by Gary Paulsen

A FINE WHITE DUST
by Cynthia Rylant

From
ATHENEUM

Published by
SIMON & SCHUSTER

BETTY G. BIRNEY

★ "Gem of a novel" —*PW*, starred review

The Seven Wonders
of Sassafras Springs

A small town boy with a severe case of wanderlust
discovers that extraordinary things aren't just
in faraway places—they can be found right next door.